01

Charmed Life

Hannah's Bright Star

Charmed Life

Caitlin's Lucky Charm

Mia's Golden Bird

Libby's Sweet Surprise

Hannah's Bright Star

Charmed Life

Hannah's Bright Star

LISA SCHROEDER

SCHOLASTIC INC.

No part of this publication may be reproduced, stored in a retrieval system, or transmitted in any form or by any means, electronic, mechanical, photocopying, recording, or otherwise, without written permission of the publisher. For information regarding permission, write to Scholastic Inc., Attention: Permissions Department, 557 Broadway, New York, NY 10012.

ISBN 978-0-545-60379-9

Text copyright © 2014 by Lisa Schroeder
All rights reserved. Published by Scholastic Inc.
SCHOLASTIC and associated logos are trademarks and/or registered trademarks of Scholastic Inc.

12 11 10 9 8 7 6 5 4 3 2   15 16 17 18 19/0

Printed in the U.S.A.   40
First printing, November 2014

Charmed Life

Hannah's Bright Star

Chapter 1

Constellation: Andromeda
Daughter of Cassiopeia

"Y'all are kidding, right?" Hannah asked as she searched under the Christmas tree for one last box. A box that would have a note in it, telling her to head out to the barn, where she would find the horse she'd always dreamed of. The horse she was absolutely, positively getting for Christmas this year.

She'd overheard her parents talking one night, as she walked by their bedroom. All right, fine, maybe she hadn't heard them mention the word *horse*, but she'd heard her mama say, "It's a pretty big responsibility. Are you sure Hannah is ready for it?"

Her daddy had assured her mama that Hannah was, indeed, ready for it, and that was all Hannah had needed to hear. After all, what other big responsibility could they have been talking about?

Her ears had been pierced since third grade.

She already owned a cell phone.

She wasn't old enough to drive.

It had to be a horse, Hannah had reasoned every single day from that night until now. It just had to be.

She crawled around the Christmas tree, pushing the mess of red, white, and green wrapping paper out of the way as she went, searching for the last box.

"Hannah," her father, Mr. Crawford, said gently, from his place on the sofa next to her mother. "There isn't another box to open. I'm sorry if you're disappointed."

With a heavy sigh, Hannah stopped looking and plopped down on the floor. She yanked on her flannel pajama top covered in penguins, straightening it out. "I am not disappointed. I'm . . . impatient. I love the gifts I've opened so far and I appreciate them, I really do, but I have a feeling there's one more. Isn't there?"

All of the gifts under the tree had been opened. The family had taken turns, to make the best part of Christmas morning last as long as possible. Her older brothers, twins Adam and Eric, were oblivious to Hannah's desperate pleas, as they had spent the last ten minutes trying to open the box that held the new video gaming system they'd received.

Hannah glanced over at her small pile of gifts that included an adorable pair of red cowboy boots, a cookie cookbook, an apron, and a necklace with an emerald pendant (her birthstone).

"Please," she begged. Hoping for some luck, Hannah fingered the charm bracelet hanging on her wrist, which she'd received from her camp friend Libby last week. "What do I have to do to get you to give it to me? I know there's one more. I just know it."

Grandpa chuckled from his place on the loveseat, next to Grandma. They lived on the same property as Hannah and her family, in the original old farmhouse, right next door. Because of their close proximity, she saw them every day, and she was thankful for that. They were two of her most favorite people in the world.

Now, Hannah eyed the two of them suspiciously. Neither of her grandparents had said a single word the past few minutes. And that wasn't like them. At all.

She made her way over to the loveseat and, while on her hands and knees, clasped her hands together out in front of her. "Grandpa, do you like seeing me crawl around here like a beggar? What do I have to do? Tell me. Please?"

He smiled as he pointed at the tree. "Say, what is that,

stuck between a couple of branches? I can't quite tell from here."

Hannah shrieked as she stood up and dashed over to the tree, stumbling over Grandpa's box of new slippers. "Where?" she cried, her hands batting at the tree branches, the scent of pine circling around her.

"Careful," her mother, Mrs. Crawford, said. "Some of those ornaments have been in my family a long time. I'd be sad to see one of them fall to the floor and break."

Something white caught Hannah's eye, tucked on a branch near the trunk, way up high. "I don't know if I can reach it," she said as she stood on her tippy-toes, stretching herself inward and upward, needles poking her cheek as she did.

And then, she had it. She grabbed whatever it was and pulled it toward her until she could see exactly what it was: an envelope.

She jumped up and down, hugging the envelope to her chest. "I knew it, I knew it!"

"What is it?" Adam asked as he brushed his long, blond bangs out of his gray-blue eyes.

"It better not be money," Eric said. "Unless there are two more envelopes just like that one stuck in there somewhere."

Adam looked at Eric. "Maybe we should look."

"It's not money," Hannah said as she tore open the envelope.

"How do you know?" Adam asked.

"I'm curious about that as well," her father mumbled.

"I just have a feeling, okay?" Hannah pulled out a purple piece of paper. "Aw, my favorite color." She unfolded the paper and read the words out loud.

There's one last gift
that's not under the tree,
so head out to the barn
where you'll squeal with glee.

Hannah dropped the purple note, grabbed her new cowboy boots, and slipped them on over her pajama bottoms. "Who's going out with me?"

"I reckon I'll go," Grandpa said as he stood up. He reached for Grandma's hand. "And I know your grandma doesn't want to miss this either."

"We'll go too," Mr. Crawford said as both he and Mrs. Crawford stood up.

Hannah clapped her hands. "You folks are slower than

maple syrup, you know that? Come on, hurry up." She looked at her brothers. "Don't you want to see what it is?"

"Not right now," Eric said.

"Yeah, maybe later," Adam said. "Mama, I'm hungry. Can we have one of Grandma's cinnamon rolls now?"

"I suppose," Mrs. Crawford replied.

"Just save some for the rest of us," Grandpa said.

"Who can eat at a time like this?" Hannah cried, grabbing her gray wool coat from the hall closet. "Let's go!"

She'd dreamed of this moment forever, it seemed.

And her dream was finally, *finally* coming true.

Chapter 2

Constellation: Equuleus the Little Horse

*H*annah fiddled with the charm bracelet as she walked toward the old, red barn, wishing and hoping for all the luck in the world right about now. She knew she shouldn't be picky, but she couldn't help wishing for the perfect horse.

Strong. Sweet. Breathtakingly beautiful.

She'd always dreamed of a golden Palomino, but she realized the chances of getting a beauty like that were slim to none, because they were usually very expensive. Still, her mind raced with the possibility.

Would it be a mare or a gelding? Hannah decided she didn't really have a preference on that.

Her grandpa, wearing his cowboy hat and old leather work boots and dressed much more sensibly than Hannah at the moment, walked ahead and opened the large wooden barn doors. Then he stepped around the corner, flipped on the lights, and came back out.

Hannah's heart raced. This was it. The moment she'd been waiting for.

Her parents and grandparents stood back, expecting Hannah to go first. She stepped inside, taking in the familiar, sweet scent of hay. Though there hadn't been a horse or hay in the barn for four or five years, the wonderful smell remained. She went to the first stall, expecting to see the horse there, but it was empty, so she continued on to the second stall.

She stopped. Stared. Blinked a few times. She looked back at her family, who seemed to be completely thrilled, as if they were about to come face-to-face with the President of the United States.

Hannah shook her head as she turned back to the stall. "I don't understand. What *is* this?"

Her grandpa stepped forward and laughed. "What do you mean, what is this?"

"Is it a . . . donkey?" Hannah asked. "I mean, it's not a horse, right? If it is, it's the strangest looking horse I've ever seen."

"No, no, it's not a donkey," Grandpa said. "It's a mule.

One of the best-trained mules in the state, I might add. You should see the ribbons this guy's racked up from the shows he's been in."

Hannah blinked the tears back. She knew she had to try and hide the disappointment she felt, because this was a gift, but it was *so* hard.

A mule? She was supposed to ride a *mule*? And be happy about it?

Her grandma stepped forward and put her arm around Hannah. "Honey, we got a real fine deal on him. He needed a good home. His previous owners wanted to find someone who would ride him and love him. We knew you could do that for him."

"That's right," Grandpa said. "His family had to move away, to Phoenix, and they couldn't take him with them. They were heartbroken about it. They worked so hard to train him. Do you know he's both a pack mule *and* a saddle mule? That shows just how special he is, that he'll happily do either. Most are one or the other."

"Please don't take this the wrong way," Hannah said, her voice quivering as she stepped back to stand by herself, "but I wanted a horse. To me it's like wanting a dog and getting a cat instead."

Her father stepped toward her and spoke sternly. "No, darlin'. It's not like that at all. This here mule can do everything a horse can do. In fact, he can do more. We did a lot of research before we pooled our money together in order to buy him for you. Besides, a mule is half horse. You know that, right?"

Hannah shrugged, because she hadn't known that. What she did know was that this animal wasn't one-hundred-percent horse, and she didn't want anything less than that.

"I think we should leave Hannah alone with him," Grandma said. "They can get to know each other a little bit without all of us standing around, gawking."

Her grandpa reached into his coat and pulled out a shiny red apple. "This ought to start things off right." He walked over and handed it to Hannah. "After we have our Christmas breakfast, you and I can come out and give him some hay, then let him out in the pen. He'll look a lot prettier in the natural light. His chestnut coat and dark brown legs are really something else when you stand back and take him in. You'll see. Oh, and we didn't tell you his name, did we? It's Bartholomew, which is a mouthful and a half, so they called him Bart for short."

Bart? Seriously?

Just when she didn't think it could get any worse. She bent her head and closed her eyes.

"Honey, you can change his name if you want," Mrs. Crawford said. "We won't mind. And I don't think Bart will either."

Hannah pinched her lips, trying hard to keep it together. She looked at her family, wondering if they expected her to come up with a name right now. How could she possibly do that when she could hardly wrap her head around what this all meant for her? She'd always imagined she'd name her first horse Dreamer. She loved the sound of it, and what it meant. But she'd never give this animal that name. Every time she'd have to say it, it would only remind her of what she *didn't* have.

"Sure. You can do that," her father said with a grin. "He's smart. I bet he'll catch on to a new name real quick."

"All right," Grandma said. "Let's go have us some cinnamon rolls. We'll see you inside in a little while, Hannah."

Once they were gone, Hannah threw the apple into the mule's stall and sat on the floor in the corner of the barn. Instead of squealing for glee like the note had said, she curled her knees up to her chest, and cried.

Chapter 3

Constellation: Coma Berenices
Berenice's Hair

*H*annah and her family spent Christmas Day with relatives who came to visit. They ate good food, played games, and watched Christmas movies. When Grandpa asked Hannah if she wanted to come with him to bring Bart in for the night, Hannah politely declined. Fortunately for her, he didn't push it.

That night, her mom came to see her after she'd gotten into bed with a book to read. "Did you have a good Christmas?" she asked Hannah.

Hannah avoided her mother's eyes as she traced the outside of the book with her finger. "I guess so."

Mrs. Crawford patted her daughter's hand. "You need to give him a chance, honey."

She didn't even have to say his name for Hannah to

know whom her mother was talking about. *Bart.* "You don't understand," Hannah said softly. "I don't know if I can."

"Well, you need to try. Listen, our receptionist at the shop is out of town for Christmas, so she won't be there tomorrow. It won't be too busy, so Grandma thought maybe you could come along and help us out. What do you say?"

Hannah's face lit up. It was exactly what she needed — to get away from here, where everyone would be bugging her to spend time with the mule. "I'd love that. What time are you leaving?"

"You should be downstairs for breakfast at eight." Mrs. Crawford stood up. "I'll call Grandpa and ask him to feed Bart in the morning and turn him out, since you're going with us, all right?"

Hannah smiled. "Thanks, Mama."

"Merry Christmas, Hannah."

"Merry Christmas."

After her mother left, Hannah set the book down and turned off the lamp, her charm bracelet jingling as she did. She burrowed down beneath the covers and thought of her three best friends from camp, Caitlin, Mia, and Libby, who shared the bracelet with Hannah, and wondered if they'd had a nice holiday. It felt like someone stuck her heart with needles, thinking about them. Boy, did she miss those girls. As she closed her eyes, all thoughts of the mule disappeared, as she recalled the laughter-filled days at Camp Brookridge.

Merry Christmas, Cabin 7 BFFs, Hannah thought as she drifted off to sleep.

The next morning, Hannah and her mother and grandmother were in the car and on their way by eight thirty-five. The plot of land Hannah's family owned was just on the outskirts of a small town called Soddy-Daisy, about twenty minutes outside Chattanooga, Tennessee. Located between the shimmering Soddy Lake and the forest-filled mountains, the town of Soddy-Daisy was both pretty and friendly. "The pretty friendly town," Hannah's father liked to joke.

Grandma and Grandpa Crawford had lived here for years, since it was where they'd raised their three sons. When Hannah's dad had proposed to her mother, he'd asked his parents if he and his bride-to-be could build a house next door. Since there was more than enough room, they'd happily agreed.

Hannah's father worked for the electric company in Chattanooga, while her mom worked as a stylist at the beauty shop Grandma owned. Beauty by Design was Grandma's baby. She'd worked hard to make it a fun and friendly place for the ladies of Soddy-Daisy. Although the shop had lots of space, she'd chosen to keep it cozy and intimate by only employing two other stylists besides herself. In the mornings, the television was usually on and tuned to the shopping channel. The stylists made fun of the featured products, like buzzards picking them apart. In the afternoons, Grandma served tea and cookies. The owner of the bakery next door, The Magic Oven, loved the Crawfords, because they bought dozens of cookies every week for their beauty shop clients.

Before every holiday, Beauty by Design was decorated as if the shop was going to be featured in a magazine. In other words, the Crawfords went all out. It was another thing that made the shop extra special.

As Grandma pulled her Toyota Avalon into the parking lot behind the shop, she said, "I just have my two Thursday regulars this morning, Gladys and Nola. What about you, Sarah?"

Hannah's mom had her appointment book in her lap. "I have two cut and colors, but I'll be done by one. It's definitely going to be a short day. Shall we all go out to lunch after we're done?"

Hannah rubbed her hands together. "Yes! Can we go to Fries and Pies? Please? Pretty please?"

The two ladies chuckled. "I wonder," her mama said, turning around and looking at her, "if you realize there *are* other restaurants in the great town of Soddy-Daisy?"

"Of course I realize that," Hannah said as she unbuckled her seat belt. "But I also know none of them even come close to being as good as Fries and Pies."

"Well," Grandma said as she opened her door. "All I can say is thank goodness they have a few salads on the menu for the over-sixteen crowd."

When they walked into the shop, Louanne, the other stylist who worked there, was snipping away on an older woman's hair. Louanne was in her thirties and had been married and divorced twice already. She was pretty, with her bleached blond hair curled around her face and her fake eyelashes plastered along her big blue eyes, but boy, did she love to talk. Grandma said her husbands probably had to divorce her in order to get some peace and quiet.

"Well good morning Nancy, Sarah, and Hannah," Louanne said, her bright red lips stretched out in a big grin. "How y'all doing? Did you have a nice Christmas?"

"We sure did," Grandma said as she walked over to her station, the first one along the wall.

Hannah went to the receptionist's desk and plopped down in the swivel chair. An itty-bitty fake Christmas tree decorated with tiny ornaments sat on the counter. A couple of little wrapped gifts were stuck underneath the tree, and Hannah wondered if they were real or just for looks.

Two women sat in the waiting area, flipping through magazines. Hannah recognized Gladys, an older lady with white, curly hair, but she wasn't sure who the other woman was. She figured it had to be her mother's first appointment. Before she could ask, her grandma kept talking.

"Hannah got quite the Christmas gift. A beautiful chestnut-colored mule named Bart, who she can ride and show."

Louanne's scissors stopped clicking. Hannah wanted to crawl under the desk and hide. Why'd her grandma have to go and say that? Knowing the way these women liked to gossip, the whole town would probably know about Hannah's mule by sunset.

"A mule?" Louanne asked, as if she might have heard wrong. "As in, one of those stubborn animals with long ears?"

"His ears aren't *that* long," Grandma said. "And he's not stubborn at all. He's got a real sweet disposition, from what we hear. Isn't that right, Hannah?"

"Mm-hmm," Hannah replied. She glanced at the two

women in the waiting area. They'd both looked up from their magazines, and were now staring at Hannah with confused looks on their faces. Fortunately, she didn't have to say anything else. Her mother walked over and said, "Good morning, Lydia. I'm ready for you."

The younger woman stood up and followed Mrs. Crawford back to her station.

"Come on over, Gladys," Grandma said. "I can't wait to hear all about your holiday."

Gladys stood up and threw the magazine she'd been looking at on the chair. "Doesn't sound like it was nearly as exciting as yours."

Hannah doodled on a note pad that sat by the phone. Yeah, to Grandma it'd be exciting. To Hannah, it was more like horrifying. What should she do about it, was the question. There was no way she was going to get up on that mule and ride him. Obviously, she couldn't return him to his original owners, since they'd moved away.

Maybe she could convince her brothers to take him on as a project. Yeah, right. After they'd heard about Bart, they hadn't even wanted to go outside and see him. Maybe after a little time went by, she could convince her parents that he'd be better off with someone else. She had to get them to understand they weren't right for each other. She just had to.

"It's almost time to start thinking about New Year's resolutions," Grandma said as she and Gladys walked over to the sink to wash Gladys's hair. "Any ideas yet, ladies?"

Grandma did this sometimes — threw out a subject for everyone in the shop to talk about. Lydia spoke up first. "I want my family to put together a float for the Valentine's Day parade. Did you hear the theme this year? Good Friends, Great Neighbors."

"I love that parade," Hannah's mom said as she stood at her counter, mixing up the color solution she would soon put on Lydia's hair. Mrs. Crawford turned and looked over at her daughter.

"Hannah, maybe you can ride Bart this year with the 4-H club! Wouldn't that be fun?"

About as fun as swimming in a lake filled with leeches, Hannah thought. She knew it was best to keep those thoughts to herself, though.

"Maybe," was all she said as she stood up from her seat. Her mother knew she'd always been envious of the girls in the club who rode their horses in the parade. It'd been a dream of hers to ride in the parade since she was a little girl.

But right now, Hannah didn't want to talk about the stupid parade. In fact, she really didn't want to talk about anything. "Grandma, can I turn on the television?"

"Sure, dear," she called out. "Go right ahead."

Hannah went over to the waiting area and searched around for the remote, stacking magazines neatly as she looked.

"Did you hear about the Weston family?" Louanne asked.

"No. What's going on?" Mrs. Crawford replied.

"It's been over six months since Tom lost his job, and they haven't been able to pay their rent the last couple of months. Rosie told me the landlord swears he's gonna have them evicted if they can't come up with the money."

"Oh, dear," Mrs. Crawford said. "How terrible. And they have all those kids too. Wherever would they go if they got put out on the street?"

Hannah knew one of those kids her mom was talking about. Her name was Elsie, and she was in the Mane Attraction 4-H club with Hannah. She was a shy and quiet girl, so they hadn't talked much. But Hannah had always liked her, because the two of them had something in common. They'd both joined in fourth grade, which was the minimum age for the club, but they'd been the only ones who didn't have a horse of their own. Owning a horse wasn't a requirement, only a love of horses, and Hannah had plenty of that.

Hannah told herself to be extra nice to Elsie at the next Mane Attraction meeting. If Hannah had gotten a horse for Christmas, like she'd wanted, she could have invited Elsie over for a ride to help cheer her up.

Well, too bad. She'd have to think of something else.

The remote was buried underneath a stack of hairstyle books. Hannah pointed it at the flat screen on the wall in the corner.

"Oh good," her mom said as the shopping channel appeared on the screen, "it's *Jewelry With Juliette*. I love her. She's absolutely adorable."

And with that, talk of the mule and the parade and Elsie's family was forgotten. Just like Hannah had hoped.

Chapter 4

CONSTELLATION: GEMINI
THE TWINS

$\mathcal{T}$hat night, at supper, Hannah poked at her meatloaf as she tried to think of an excuse to get out of feeding Bart and putting him in the barn for the night.

"You all right, Hannah?" her mother asked.

She felt everyone's eyes on her all of a sudden. "I don't know," Hannah said softly. "Not feeling very well, I guess."

Mrs. Crawford wiped her mouth with the napkin and put it back in her lap. "You had a real good appetite at lunch. Pretty sure I've never seen a girl eat as many fries as you did."

"Aw, man," Adam said. "Did you guys go to Fries and Pies without us?"

"Yep. Sorry, boys," Mrs. Crawford said. "I'll have to take you two another time. You want to come to the beauty shop with me tomorrow and help out, like Hannah did today?"

They both wrinkled their noses. "You're kidding, right?" Eric said. "Not in a hundred years."

Mr. Crawford chuckled. "Well, that's good. I was counting on you boys taking care of that squeaky pen gate tomorrow. Grandpa said he'd help, since I'll be at work." He turned to Hannah, reaching out and putting his big, calloused hand against her forehead. "You don't feel warm. Just got a stomachache, darlin'?"

"Yeah," Hannah said. "Can I be excused? Think I'll go lie down for a while."

"All right, but you should take care of Bart first. It'll only take a few minutes."

Hannah sighed. "Can you do it for me, Daddy? Please?"

Mr. Crawford leaned back in his chair and looked hard at his daughter. "Hannah, why do I get the feeling you're doing your very best to avoid that mule? This isn't how it works. We gave him to you. He's your responsibility."

"I know, but I —"

"You realize you could work with him to do whatever class you'd like for shows, right?" Mrs. Crawford said. "Single driving, halter, even barrels. He's good, Hannah. You'll see."

"He could do all of those and more, in *one* show," Mr. Crawford said, turning back to his plate of food. "That's the great thing about mules. Horses need to be more specialized, but mules are smart and don't tire as easily." He took a bite of mashed potatoes and gravy, then turned to Hannah. "One thing is for sure. That mule needs to get to work. Soon. He's not meant to stand around, day after day, doing nothing."

Now Hannah's stomach really did hurt. She didn't want to ride Bart, or work with him, or show him. When would her parents realize they could talk for hours about how great Bart was, but that didn't mean Hannah was going to suddenly change her mind about him?

No. Her mind was made up. She pushed her chair back from the table and stood up. "I'm going to my room. If you could please take care of Bart, Daddy, I'd really appreciate it."

"Hannah —"

She didn't wait to hear what he had to say, but instead rushed up the stairs, her hand clutched to her stomach. Maybe it was rude, but she just couldn't handle any more talk about Bart right now.

When she got to her room, she sat at her desk and picked up the letter from Caitlin she'd received earlier that day. In the letter, Caitlin had talked about her plans for winter break, which included lots of fun activities with her new friends, Esther and Tezra. She'd asked about Hannah's plans, and had told her to write to her as soon as she could, to tell her all about her new horse.

Hannah leaned back in her chair and sighed. She had written to all three of her camp friends and told them she was getting a horse for Christmas. What a stupid thing to do. Now she'd have to write to each of them and tell them about what had really happened. Either that, or lie, and she really didn't want to do that.

She opened a drawer and pulled out one of the cute note cards she'd gotten for Christmas from her best friend in Soddy-Daisy, Crystal. This particular card had an adorable pig on it along with the words "Hogs and Kisses." Crystal was out of town, visiting her grandparents, and wouldn't be back for another week. They'd exchanged Christmas gifts before she'd left, just like they'd done every year since they'd met in second grade. Hannah opened the card and started writing.

Dear Caitlin,

It's the day after Christmas, and I keep wishing for a do-over of yesterday. Okay, so the cinnamon rolls Grandma made were fabulous, like always. My five boy cousins were annoying, like always. We played games all afternoon and by the end of the day, I just wanted to disappear to my small but peaceful bedroom and read a book.

But here's where things went really, really wrong. There was an envelope tucked into the branches of the Christmas tree. It told me to head out to the barn for my last gift. Yes, yes, I know what you're thinking, because it's what I thought too. It has to be the horse, right?

Wrong.

They didn't get me a horse. They got me a mule. My daddy told me, he's half a horse, like that's supposed to make it okay. Well, it's not okay with me. I'm trying to understand why they did it, but I honestly don't understand. They tell me he needed a good home. Well, I bet there are a lot of horses out there that could use a good home too. They tell me he's a blue-ribbon winner and he's got a sweet disposition and all this other stuff, and all I can think about is that it's a mule they're talking about, so why does it matter?

To them, it doesn't matter, but to me it matters so much. I don't know what to do. It's not like an ugly sweater that can be returned to the store, you know? The people who sold him to my family moved away. They're gone.

And I'm stuck with Bart. Yeah, that's his name — Bart. Nice, right? Not.

I sure hope your Christmas was better than mine. At least I have the bracelet to wear, and I love it so much. When I put it on after I got it last week, do you know what memory popped up? You won't believe it. It was the evil squirrel, running toward me. I swear that squirrel is going to haunt me for the rest of my life.

I miss you, Caitlin! I'm glad it's almost the new year because in that new year, I'll get to see you again and I cannot wait! Please write back when you get the chance.

Your Cabin 7 BFF,
Hannah

Chapter 5

Constellation: Crater
the Cup

The next morning, Hannah was downstairs by eight, hoping her mother would let her go to the salon again.

Mrs. Crawford was in the kitchen, filling up her mug with coffee. "Morning, Mama," Hannah said as she went to the fridge to get the carton of orange juice.

"You feeling better?" she asked Hannah before she took a sip of her coffee.

"Yes, and I was hoping I could go to work with you again today," Hannah said as she poured the juice.

"I suppose it's all right. It'll be busier than yesterday. We'll be there most of the day."

"Fine with me," Hannah said. "Not much to do around here anyway. Crystal doesn't get back until next week."

"You know, you could spend some time —"

"Mama, please don't," Hannah said as she put the juice back in the fridge. "I know what you're going to say, and I think maybe I just need a little bit more time to get used to the idea, all right? Please don't be upset with me. Please?"

"I'm trying to understand," her mother replied. "We all are. But you need to put in a little effort too, I think."

Hannah went to the pantry and pulled out a box of cereal bars. "Can you call Grandpa and ask if he can take care of him again? Just for today."

"Hannah, this really has to stop. You're not even giving Bart a chance."

She didn't understand what it was like for Hannah. None of her family did. Bart wasn't what Hannah had wanted, at all, and spending time with him wasn't going to change her mind.

"It's not fair," Hannah said softly as she slowly pulled one of the bars from the box, avoiding her mother's eyes. "He's not what I wanted."

"Look at me, young lady."

Hannah set the box on the counter and did as she was told.

"I'm sorry you're disappointed. But until you give him a chance, there's nothing to discuss. You're spending all your time trying to avoid him, based on things you've made up in your mind, rather than getting to know him. You think you've been treated unfairly, but I say, Bart is the one being treated unfairly in this situation."

"But Mama, I just don't . . . I don't think he's the right animal for me."

Mrs. Crawford threw her arm up in the air, clearly exasperated. "You don't even know him!"

Hannah bowed her head. She could tell this was a war she couldn't win. She had to at least look like she was putting in some effort. "Fine," she said, meeting her mother's eyes again. "I'll take care of him tomorrow. But there isn't time now, if I'm going with you to the shop."

Her mother narrowed her eyes. "You really mean it?"

Hannah crossed her heart with her finger. "I promise. Tomorrow it'll be Bart and me. You'll see."

Mrs. Crawford sighed. "All right. I believe you." She took a long swig of coffee. "Oh, I meant to tell you, Mr. Brody called last night after you went up to your room. He wanted to talk about the New Year's Eve party for the Mane Attraction Club."

Mr. Brody was their 4-H leader. Hannah and the other kids really liked him. He'd worked around horses most of his life, but was retired now. He said the 4-H club was a way for him to stay connected to the world of horses that he loved so much.

"Oh yeah," Hannah said. "He was supposed to let us know where the party would be held. What'd he decide?"

"Well, that's why he called. He asked if we'd be willing to host it here."

"Oh no," Hannah said. "You didn't agree to that, did you?"

Her mother shook her head, confused. "What's wrong with having it here? I told him I didn't mind at all. I offered up the barn, since there's plenty of room out there, and you kids can be as loud as you want to be."

"The barn? Are you kidding me? Mama, I think that's a terrible idea."

"It's not terrible," she said as she went to the fridge and pulled out the carton of eggs. "It'll be great, you'll see. We'll set up tables for food and take the laptop out there so you can play music. Mr. Brody said he'd come up with games for you guys to play throughout the night."

Hannah munched on her cereal bar as she paced the kitchen. She'd already decided she wouldn't say anything about the mule to the kids in the club. But if they came here, they'd see him for sure.

It was like her mother could read her mind. "Honey, are you afraid they'll make fun of you because you have a mule instead of a horse?"

She stopped pacing. "Yes. Yes, I am. I mean, it's a horse club, isn't it? Not a mule club."

"But you can still ride him like a horse. Show him like a horse. I think they'll understand, when you explain why we did it. You know, they might even think it's cool, having something that's a little bit different. Who knows, maybe you'll make mules the next big thing."

"I really don't think so," Hannah said under her breath as she shoved the rest of the cereal bar into her mouth. She washed it down with orange juice.

Her mother cracked four eggs into the frying pan and scrambled them up with a whisk. "Well, you should try to be excited when you introduce Bart to your friends. If you're excited, they'll be excited."

"Can we please call Mr. Brody back and ask him to find somewhere else to have the party?" Hannah asked. "I really don't think it'll be very fun here. I mean, last year we met at Lazerport and played laser tag and video games all night. This party will be so lame compared to that."

Her mother turned from her eggs for a moment and looked sternly at Hannah. "He's trying to keep costs down

32

this year. Unfortunately, not everyone has the money for things like laser tag and video games."

Hannah felt her cheeks get warm, and she instantly felt bad. She'd forgotten about Elsie's financial situation. Of course Elsie wouldn't be able to spend money at a party. Having it at someone's house did make the most sense in terms of cost.

Her mom continued, as she went back to cooking the scrambled eggs, "We'll do everything we can to make it fun, I promise. And as far as Bart is concerned, everyone probably knows about him by now anyway. You know how things spread around our little town."

"Yeah, I know," Hannah said. "Like wildfire. Or a contagious disease. Or . . ." Her voice trailed off.

Her mother laughed. "Can't think of another one to compare it to?"

"Nope. Oh well. You really think everyone already knows?"

"I sure do. Can you get a couple of plates, so we can eat these eggs?" her mother asked. "Grandma will be here shortly."

Hannah went to the cupboard and pulled out two plates. "My life would be so much easier if you'd just gotten me a regular horse, like I wanted."

As her mother put some eggs on each plate, she said, "And since when, may I ask, is life supposed to be easy?"

"Is this where you tell me I need to make lemonade out of lemons?"

"No, I won't tell you that," she said with a smile, patting Hannah's arm as she walked toward the kitchen table, "because you just said it. Though that is exactly what you need to do, my dear, sweet daughter."

Chapter 6

Constellation: Volans
Flying Fish

*T*he next morning, Hannah did as she'd promised. She went out to the barn, fed Bart some hay, and when he was finished, attached a lead rope to his halter and took him to the outside pen.

"Just so you know, I'm sorry about this," Hannah said as she walked with him. "I mean, I'm sorry you ended up somewhere you don't belong. And that's really all I have to say to you."

She turned and looked at him and saw that his ears were forward, like he was listening intently. As she unclipped the lead, he gave her the slightest of nudges with his muzzle. A friendly one, as if to say, *It's all right.*

He didn't give her a bit of trouble that day, or the following days, either. After she talked to Bart that first day, she didn't say another word to him. And she refused to pet him or give him any affection. This was temporary, she told herself. Soon, everyone would see the two weren't a good match and they'd sell Bart and get Hannah what she'd wanted all along — a beautiful horse.

When the day of the New Year's Eve party arrived, Mrs. Crawford and Hannah went out to the barn to figure out what they needed to do to get ready.

"I have a surprise for you," Hannah's mother told her as she opened the barn doors.

After the disappointment of Christmas Day, Hannah knew better than to get her hopes up. "Let me guess," she said. "I get to clean out Bart's stall again."

Her mom laughed, then pointed toward the other end of the barn. "You know that for years, we've kept the hayloft closed off to you kids. It needed repairs we just didn't want to deal with. But this past week, your father had someone come out and do the work. It's a fantastic space, and the perfect place for your party tonight."

Hannah looked at her mother. "We get to go upstairs? Really?"

"Yes, really."

Hannah clapped her hands together. "Oh my gosh, this

is *so* exciting. Do you know when I was like six or seven, Adam and Eric had me convinced you were stashing dead bodies up there?"

Her mom shuddered. "Hannah, no! That's terrible. What kind of people do you think we are?"

"Hey, don't get upset with *me*. Talk to my mean older brothers who loved to torture me every chance they got. I'm pretty sure there was an entire year where I kept my room immaculate because I was scared of what might happen if I didn't."

Her mom laughed again. "Oh, dear. I hope you didn't tell your friends about your suspicions."

"Yeah, that was also the year I didn't have any friends over to play. You mean you didn't notice?"

They reached the end of the barn, and where there was nothing before, there was now a set of stairs for climbing up to the hayloft.

"Where'd they come from?" Hannah asked.

"They were folded up into the trapdoor in the ceiling. Pull on the rope, open the trapdoor, and stairs magically appear."

"Wow," Hannah said. "That's like something out of *Minecraft*. You know, that game?"

Her mom smiled. "Well, clearly, the builders of this barn were way ahead of their time."

"I can't believe I finally get to see what's up there."

"After you," her mom said, waving her arm toward the stairs.

Hannah climbed until her head reached the loft, then she stopped and peered around. At the far end of the barn was the large window that her grandpa called the hay hole. He'd explained to her that hay bales were brought into the loft through that hole by way of a hay elevator. Since it was wintertime and not exactly warm outside, it was closed up. There were small windows up near the roof, though, that provided some light.

In the corner, to Hannah's immediate right, was something she couldn't quite make out. "What is that big thing in the corner?" she called down to her mother.

"Climb up and take a look!" her mother called as she made her way up the stairs.

So Hannah went ahead and climbed all the way up, until she was standing in the loft. The thing she'd wondered about had a wooden platform with a few stairs, so she went closer and only then could she finally see what she couldn't see before.

"Mama, seriously? A trampoline?"

Her mother stood behind her now. "Yes. Isn't it just so fun? Your grandpa and a few of his friends built it up here many years ago, for his three young boys to play on."

"How come you're just now telling me about it?" Hannah asked.

"Well, because one of the springs broke and no one ever had it fixed. It was the New Year's Eve party that pushed your daddy to finally get it done."

"Can I try it out?" Hannah asked.

"Sure! Go right ahead. You'll notice the mat is woven, which is different from today's trampolines. And the springs are nice and big, so you'll bounce really high. Stay away from the edges, all right?"

Someone had piled bales of hay around the platform so you couldn't fall, but Hannah could see that what her mother was mostly concerned about were the big gaps between the springs, especially in the corners.

Hannah jumped, higher and higher, until it felt like she was flying. For fifteen minutes, she jumped, until she was out of breath. When she stepped off, her mama said, "I haven't seen you smile that much in a long time."

"It's fun!" Hannah said. "The kids are gonna love it. Can we jump in groups?"

"Probably no more than two at a time. Safest that way. Now come on, we have a lot of work to do. Let's go get your brothers to help us haul the folding tables and lights and other things we need to put up here for the party."

Hannah looked around and thought maybe it wasn't such a bad place to have a New Year's Eve party after all. That is, until she walked by Bart, and all of her anxiety came rushing back.

Chapter 7

Constellation: Horologium
the Clock

Hannah's mother was right. All the kids in the Mane Attraction 4-H club had heard about the mule. Word had gotten around, no thanks to her grandma, who'd probably told everyone who came into the beauty shop the past week.

There were nine kids coming to the party, and once they'd all arrived, around eight o'clock, Hannah and her parents along with Mr. Brody took the group out to the barn. Of course, everyone wanted to see Bart.

Hannah's grandpa and father had strung Christmas lights all around the barn, giving it a fun, festive look. They also helped to brighten up the place, since the few light fixtures in the barn didn't give off a ton of light. The kids *oohed* and *ahhed* as they walked in.

When the group got to Bart's stall, everyone stood there and stared at him. Darren, one of only two boys in the club, said, "Can we take turns riding him? I want to see if it's any different from riding a horse. It has to be, right? I mean, he looks different, he must ride different too."

"Yeah, he looks weird," Carson, the other boy, said.

"Hey, now," Mr. Brody said. "Come on, that ain't nice. Didn't your mama teach you, if you can't say something nice, don't say anything at all?"

"Well, I think he's beautiful," Mary Beth said as she twirled a strand of her red hair around her finger. "And look at those eyes. When he looked at me, I swear, it was like he could see into the deepest part of my soul."

Hannah glanced over at Elsie and rolled her eyes. Mary Beth was a sophomore in high school and she was like a walking, talking love poem.

"We're not going to ride Bart tonight," Mr. Crawford said, stepping forward. "We have other things planned. Did y'all know we have a trampoline in our hayloft?"

The kids looked at each other with surprise.

"No way," Carson said.

"Yes, way," Mr. Crawford replied. "Come on. I'll show you!"

"Be careful going up those stairs," Mrs. Crawford called out.

While everyone else went up to check out the trampoline, Hannah hung back, trying to shake off Carson's nasty comment. She told herself it shouldn't bother her. After all, wasn't that sort of what she thought every time she looked at Bart?

"I like him," a soft voice said. "Your mule, I mean."

Hannah turned to find Elsie still standing there. Her long brown bangs were braided and pulled back, making her brown eyes behind her glasses stand out a lot more. She usually kind of hid behind those bangs.

"You do?" Hannah asked. "I like your hair, by the way."

"Thanks. And yeah, I think he's real pretty. I noticed his legs are darker than the rest of him. You don't see that very often."

"So, you don't think he's . . . weird?" Hannah asked.

Elsie smiled. "No. Just because he's different doesn't mean he's weird."

"It doesn't?" Hannah asked, although as the words came out she realized she actually already knew the answer to this question.

"Okay, look at Tanya Lovelace," Elsie explained. "No one in country music has ever captured the thoughts and feelings of girls the way her music does. Is that weird? No, it's just different. I wish people would stop thinking of different as being strange, you know? If we all looked the same and acted the same and talked the same, wouldn't that be boring?"

Hannah nodded her head slowly. "It makes a lot of sense, when you say it like that."

"My mama always says I'm a very sensible person."

Hannah laughed. "You're also pretty quiet. I think this is the most I've ever heard you talk."

"I have a big family and they don't let me talk much," Elsie said as she walked closer to the stall, her eyes glued to Bart the entire time. "I guess I forget that not everyone is like that. You know, you're really lucky, Hannah. I'd be jumping for joy if he were mine. I bet he rides like a dream, doesn't he?"

Hannah looked down at her red cowboy boots. "Actually, I haven't ridden him yet."

"You haven't?" Elsie asked, her eyes big like an owl's. "How come?"

Hannah shrugged. "Wasn't very excited to, I guess. I really wanted a horse, you know? I mean, it's all I ever dreamed about, and then I walked out here and found Bart."

"He's better than nothing, isn't he?" Elsie asked as she stroked Bart's muzzle.

Hannah didn't answer that.

"Can I ride him?" Elsie asked. "Not tonight, since the party's going on, but maybe this weekend? I can try him out for you, if you're scared. I don't mind at all."

"Hannah," Mr. Crawford yelled from the loft. "You coming up soon?"

"Yeah, I'll be up in a minute," Hannah called back. She looked at Elsie again. "I guess you could come over Saturday. If you're sure you really want to."

"I really, really do," Elsie said. "Now come on. We better get up there. You know, because there's only three and a half hours left until the clock strikes midnight. We might miss it."

Hannah laughed again. Then she asked, "Do you think it's going to be a good year?"

As they approached the stairs, Elsie stopped walking and said, "All I can say is, I hope it's better than this stupid, lousy year."

For Elsie's sake, Hannah hoped so too.

Chapter 8

Constellation: Pegasus
the Winged Horse

Saturday afternoon, Hannah's phone beeped, letting her know someone wanted to video chat. She picked it up and squealed when she saw Crystal's name.

"Hey! Are you home?" Hannah asked as she looked at Crystal's freckled face on the screen of her phone. Her thick, brown hair was extra curly (and frizzy) today.

"Yes, ma'am, I sure am," Crystal said with a smile.

Hannah had told her not to call her ma'am hundreds of times, but it didn't do any good. Her parents were big believers in manners, and Crystal got carried away sometimes.

"I'm sorry I didn't call while we were gone," she continued. "Mama took away my phone. Said I was on it too much when I should be spending time with the family."

"It's fine," Hannah said. "I totally understand. Did you have a good Christmas?"

"Oh yeah, it was awesome. I got new boots. Super cute blue ones."

Hannah gasped. "I got red ones! I love them to pieces."

"Yeah? But that's not all you got, right? Tell me, Hannah, please. Tell me all about him. Or her. I want to know everything. When Mama handed my phone back to me, I was shocked that you hadn't sent me any pictures yet."

Clearly, there was no getting out of it. Before Crystal had left, Hannah had told her about the conversation she'd heard between her parents, sure as the sky is blue that she'd be getting a horse for Christmas. "Well, things didn't turn out quite the way I thought they were going to," Hannah said.

Crystal narrowed her eyes. "What does that even mean? You didn't get a horse? What'd you get, then?"

Hannah sighed, then said it quickly, to get it over with. "A mule."

Crystal wrinkled her face. "A what?"

"A mule," Hannah repeated. "His name is Bart. They got him from a family who had to move to Arizona. I guess he's won a bunch of ribbons and —"

"Hannah, wait," Crystal interrupted. "You can't be serious."

"Yep. Serious as the evening news."

"Well, can you, like, exchange him? For something better? I mean, it just doesn't seem fair. How come they didn't ask you first, before they went and did that?"

"I don't know," Hannah said, falling back on to her bed, holding her phone above her. "I guess they didn't think I'd mind that he's different. I told them that to me, it's like asking for a dog and getting a cat instead. Not everyone thinks it's strange, though. Elsie loves him. She's actually coming over to ride him in a little while."

"Elsie?" Crystal asked. "That shy girl from 4-H?"

"Yeah. We had the New Year's Eve party here, so she got to see him. Honest and true, she thinks Bart's the best thing since the Snickers bar."

"Maybe you should give him to her."

"Yeah, I don't think my family would let me do that. Besides . . ." She almost told her about Elsie's family's financial problems, but decided she'd better not. The last thing she wanted was to be like Louanne, spreading gossip around town like it was good for you. "Never mind," she muttered.

"Well, what *are* you gonna do, then?"

Hannah sat up and ran her fingers through her long, straight hair. "I don't know. I just keep hoping some brilliant idea will come to me one of these days. I better go. Elsie should be here any minute. See you at school on Monday, I guess."

"You know it. Wear your new boots, please. I want to see them."

"All right, I will. Bye."

"Bye."

Hannah went downstairs and found Mr. Crawford at the table, having some coffee and cookies.

"Daddy, Elsie's coming over any minute, and she wants to ride Bart. Think you could help me saddle him up?"

He smiled, his dark blue eyes practically twinkling. He stroked his scruffy beard and said, "Why, that's the best news I've had all day, darlin'. Been waiting for you to ask me. He's got a real nice saddle that his other family gave us." He finished his cookie and stood up. "I'll go out now and bring him in from the pen and get him ready. When Elsie arrives, you girls come on out and join me, all right?"

"Okay. Thanks for doing that."

He gave Hannah a hug and said, "My pleasure."

After he left, Hannah helped herself to the last cookie from the cookie jar, thinking about Crystal's reaction after hearing about Bart. She hadn't even asked Hannah if she liked him or not, just crinkled up her face and suggested

Hannah try and get rid of him. It kind of hurt Hannah's feelings, but hadn't that pretty much been Hannah's reaction? Still, it bothered her.

When Elsie arrived a little while later, they went out to the barn and found Hannah's dad riding Bart.

He waved at the two of them. "I haven't told you this, Hannah, but I've ridden him a few times already. Wanted to make sure he'd be easy for you to handle in these new surroundings, and he hasn't given me a lick of trouble."

"Well, that's good," Hannah said. She looked at Elsie. "Are you sure you want to do this?"

"Are you kidding?" Elsie said. "I can't wait!"

Mr. Crawford rode Bart out to the small corral while Hannah and Elsie followed along. "Gosh, I just think he looks so pretty," Elsie said. "I even love his roached mane."

Hannah looked at her. "You mean, how it's clipped super short?"

"Yeah. Looks nice and tidy. The only thing that bothers me is he doesn't look like a Bart. Have you thought of changing his name?"

"Yeah, my parents said I could change it if I wanted to. I just haven't thought about it that much, to be honest."

"The right name will come to you," Elsie said. "Just wait and see."

Once they were in the corral, Mr. Crawford brought Bart to a stop and hopped down. Elsie went around to the mule's left side, put her foot in the stirrup, and mounted Bart like a pro. "You look like you know what you're doing," he said. "You ride quite a bit, then?"

"Not as much as I'd like to. We've got one horse at home. With seven kids, we have to take turns. I ride once a week or so." Elsie bent down over the saddle horn and gave Bart's neck a nice rub. "All right, Mister. You ready to do this thing with me?"

Elsie held the reins like she was ready to go and squeezed her legs against Bart's sides, which got him to start walking. Hannah and her father stepped out of the corral, so they wouldn't be in the way. They leaned up against the railing and watched Elsie and Bart walk around the circle.

After a few minutes of walking, Elsie clicked her tongue a couple of times, gave a little kick of her feet, and the mule started trotting.

Hannah was mesmerized. Bart looked incredible. Not only that, Elsie was grinning from ear-to-ear, and she looked so comfortable, like she'd been riding him forever. Pretty soon, she had him break out into a nice canter.

Around and around they went, until finally, Elsie pulled on the reins and with a gentle "Whoa," brought him to a stop.

She dismounted as Mr. Crawford and Hannah came back into the corral. "He rides like a dream," Elsie said. "Almost felt like we were flying through the air there for a minute. Hannah, I promise, you have nothing to be scared of. He's amazing. You have to ride him. You just have to."

"Do you want to, darlin'?" Mr. Crawford asked. "Seems like the perfect time to give him a try."

Maybe so, but he wasn't the perfect horse Hannah had dreamed about forever. "No thanks," Hannah said. She looked at Elsie. "Want to go inside and make some cookies? I got a new cookie cookbook for Christmas, and since I ate the last cookie earlier, seems only right I bake some new ones."

"Only if you'll come home with me when we're done baking and have supper at our place. My mother told me to invite you to come over tonight."

"Is that all right, daddy?" Hannah asked him.

"Fine with me," he said. "What kind of cookies you girls gonna bake?"

Hannah took Elsie's arm and pulled her toward the house. "It's a surprise," she yelled back to Mr. Crawford, thinking back to the surprise she was so excited about at Christmas time, and how her family had crushed those dreams in an instant. "Something you'll never expect."

"So, what are we making, exactly?" Elsie whispered.

"Peanut butter," Hannah said with a smile. "My brothers' favorite, while my daddy only likes them a little bit. We'll just see how he likes them apples."

"Wait," Elsie said, looking confused. "We're putting apples into the peanut butter cookies?"

It made Hannah laugh, all the way to the kitchen.

Chapter 9

CONSTELLATION: Orion
the Hunter

"Hey, kids, time to dish up!" a male voice bellowed from upstairs. Elsie and Hannah were down in the basement at Elsie's house along with some of her brothers and sisters, watching reruns of *The Lacy Bell Show*. Hannah had told everyone that her camp friend Mia, who lived in Southern California, was a friend of Lacy's. They'd all thought that was pretty neat.

As the kids scurried up the stairs, Elsie explained to Hannah that everyone dished up in the kitchen, because it was easier that way with such a large group of people. Then they'd take their plates and find a seat at the table in the dining room.

The smell of onions and garlic got stronger as they approached the kitchen. "Mmm, smells good," Hannah said.

"Yep. It's spaghetti night," Elsie told Hannah.

In the kitchen, kids were grabbing plates and scooping up salad, spaghetti, and slices of bread. It was crowded and chaotic, but not in a bad way. In the best way, actually. Even though Hannah had only been there less than an hour, it felt comfy and cozy. Like a home.

Hannah followed Elsie's lead and once they'd made their way around the kitchen and filled their plates, they went to the dining room and took a seat at the huge dining room table.

Hannah sat down next to one of the younger girls, while Elsie sat on the other side of Hannah.

"What's your name?" the girl asked. Hannah looked over at her and wondered how old she was. Five? Six, maybe? One of the older brothers poured milk into the girl's cup and then passed the pitcher to Hannah.

"My name's Hannah. What's yours?"

"I'm Minnie. Like the mouse."

"Nice to meet you, Minnie." Hannah said as she poured herself some milk into a plastic cup that wasn't very big. She glanced around and saw that everyone had the same small cups. Elsie reached over and took the pitcher from Hannah.

"One glass of milk for everyone," Elsie told Hannah, leaning in so she could hear her over the buzzing of conversation. "After that, if you're thirsty, you can get up and help yourself to water. There's ice in the freezer."

"Okay, thanks." Hannah suddenly felt guilty being there. Probably the last thing this family needed was another mouth to feed. She kicked herself for taking any milk at all.

"All right, quiet now," Elsie's father, Mr. Weston, said from his spot at the head of the table. Hannah noticed that he and his three sons all had buzz cuts, so they kind of looked alike. One thing about Mr. Weston that stood out to Hannah as he reached over and took his wife's and son's hands in his — he had some of the biggest hands she'd ever seen. Minnie reached over and held Hannah's hand, while Elsie took the other one. Everyone bowed their heads, so Hannah did the same.

"Heavenly Father," Mr. Weston said, "we give thanks to you this day. We ask that you please bless this food, our family, and our friends who are dining with us today. Amen."

"Amen," everyone repeated.

And then, hands went quickly from holding to eating, as everyone dove into their plates of food.

"So tell us, Elsie, how was the mule?" Mr. Weston asked. "What's his name again?"

"His name is Bart, for now," Elsie said as she finished taking a drink of milk. "Hannah still might change it. Anyway, he has the sweetest personality. I loved riding him. Didn't give me any trouble at all."

Mr. Weston smiled as he twirled his spaghetti around and around on his fork. "Well, that's good to hear. And what about you, Sally? How was your afternoon babysitting for the Tuckers?"

"It was fine, I guess," Sally said. She sat across from Hannah and looked to be a few years older than Elsie. "The toddler went down for his nap just fine, but that baby boy did not want anything to do with his crib. So I turned on the radio, sat in the rocking chair, and I just held him the whole time. Didn't get a single word read in the book I'd brought along."

Mr. Weston chuckled. "I reckon your mama can relate to that."

"Sometimes babies just want nothing more than to be held," Mrs. Weston replied. "I'm glad you obliged, Sally. That was the right thing to do."

As Hannah ate her spaghetti, which was delicious, she looked around at the kind and friendly faces of the Weston family. It made her heart hurt thinking about them getting kicked out of their home. She had this urge to ask them about it, to find out if maybe things had magically turned around somehow in the past week, but she knew that would be rude. So she just kept her thoughts to herself as she ate her supper.

When everyone was finished, Hannah followed Elsie into the kitchen, carrying her dishes. "Just set them here, on the counter," Elsie said. "Thankfully, it's not my turn to wash them, so we can go do something." She glanced at Hannah and grinned. "Want to see one of my favorite things to do after the sun goes down?"

Hannah raised her eyebrows. "I don't know. Do I?"

Elsie laughed. "Yes, you do. Come on. Follow me."

"Thank you for having me for supper, ma'am," Hannah said to Mrs. Weston as the two girls weaved through the bodies in the kitchen. "It was really good."

"You're welcome," she replied, looking down at Hannah with her warm brown eyes. "It was a pleasure having you join us. Come back anytime."

With the pleasantries out of the way, Hannah followed Elsie away from the chaos of the kitchen and toward the front door. There was a coatrack in the entryway, and Elsie grabbed her own coat along with Hannah's and handed it to her. Then, Elsie went to the hall closet and took down two pairs of binoculars and two flashlights that hung from hooks on the door.

Once they'd stepped outside into the cool night air, Elsie bent her head back and took in a deep breath.

"You okay?" Hannah asked.

"I love my family, but I also love getting away from them sometimes." Elsie reached over and hung a pair of binoculars around Hannah's neck, then handed her a flashlight. "Come on. This way. We have to go out to the middle of the field for the best view."

They crossed the gravel road in front of the two-story house and made their way to the grassy field. The sky was clear, with just a sliver of a moon hanging there. The two girls pointed their flashlights at the ground, to help them see where they were going. Hannah wasn't sure what they'd be able to see in the darkness, but it seemed like Elsie knew what she was doing, so Hannah didn't say anything, just followed along behind her.

After they'd walked a ways, Elsie stopped, looked up, and said, "Okay, this is far enough." She clicked off her flashlight and stuck it in her coat pocket, so Hannah did the same.

"You know anything about stargazing?" Elsie asked.

"No," Hannah said. "I mean, my grandpa's pointed out the Big Dipper to me before. But that's about it."

"Did you know that if you find the Big Dipper, you've also found part of the Big Bear too? It's not as easy to find, though. My daddy says that ancient Greeks and Romans believed that a mythological king grabbed the bear's tail and swung it into the sky."

"Wow," Hannah said. "Are there other stories like that?"

"Oh yeah," Elsie said. "Tons of them. There are eighty-eight constellations. I have books about them and I come out here and try to find them, according to the month that it's easiest to find them. Tonight I thought I'd try and show you Orion, the Hunter. You've heard of that one, right?"

"No."

"He's pretty easy to find in the winter because of his belt, which is made up of three stars." She put the binoculars to her eyes and after a few seconds pointed to her left. "There. See the three stars kind of close together? That's his belt."

"Yeah," Hannah said, smiling. "I see them."

They peered through their binoculars for a while, as Elsie pointed out the other stars that made up the shape of Orion. When she was done, Hannah asked her, "So how come you like this so much? Stargazing, I mean?"

"I guess because the stars, all sparkly and pretty, feel magical to me." Elsie paused and looked at Hannah. "I wish on stars every night, hoping I can have a little bit of their magic myself. But even if I can't, I feel pretty lucky to be able to stand here and breathe the fresh air and watch this magical sky." She raised her binoculars again. "Yep. We're real lucky, Hannah. That's for sure."

Chapter 10

CONSTELLATION: Crux
the Cross

$\mathcal{S}$unday morning, as she sat at the table with a bagel and a glass of juice, Hannah fingered her charm bracelet, thinking about what Elsie had said. *We're real lucky.* Even though there was a big possibility Elsie's family might get kicked out of their house, she considered herself lucky.

That was pretty remarkable.

After wearing the bracelet and wishing so hard for a horse, and getting Bart instead, Hannah wasn't so sure anymore that the bracelet was lucky. It seemed her camp friends still believed it was, though, so she decided she shouldn't be so quick to think the worst.

"You about ready?" her mama asked, before she took one last drink of coffee and set the mug in the kitchen sink.

"Yep," Hannah said as she stood up, smoothing out her skirt. "I'm ready."

Hannah was going to the early church service with her grandma and mother, and after that, they'd be working at the beauty shop for a couple hours. There were a few clients who worked jobs that didn't allow them to get to Beauty by Design any other day of the week. So, the first weekend of every month, the shop was open on both Saturday and Sunday.

Church was the usual routine of singing, preaching, and praying. Hannah's grandma hurried out the doors when it was over, with Hannah and her mother not far behind.

When they got in the car, Mrs. Crawford said, "That was a good sermon. It's so important to remember to count our blessings all through the year, not just during the holiday season."

"The first thing I say every morning is *thank you for this day*," Grandma said. "Every day's a gift. Right, Hannah?"

Grandma glanced at Hannah in the rearview mirror. "Right," Hannah said, because what else was there to say, really? "You know, when I was at Elsie's house yesterday, you'd never guess that they're having troubles."

"Well, that's wonderful," Grandma said. "From what I've seen over the years, sure seems like nothing good ever comes from moping around about your problems. Best to try and find the bright side somehow, some way."

Hannah wondered if her grandma was talking about the situation with Bart, specifically. It sort of seemed like it. Except Hannah wasn't moping around. Not really. Although she wasn't really trying to find the bright side, either. Mostly, she just tried not to think about him as much as possible. It was easier that way.

When Hannah, her mother, and her grandmother walked into Beauty by Design, Louanne had the radio blasting and was singing along as she swept the floor. Her back was to the front door, so she didn't see them come in.

Hannah's grandma marched right over to the radio and turned it down. "My word, are we running a beauty shop or *America's Got Talent*?"

Louanne looked a little shocked, but she recovered quickly. "Good morning to you too Nancy. We don't have any clients coming in for another twenty minutes or so. I figured I'd have a little fun. Whistle while I work, so to speak."

"But you weren't whistling," Grandma said under her breath. It made Hannah smile. She knew her grandma didn't really mean anything by it. She was probably just a little cranky about having to come to work on a Sunday. Although she loved her little salon, there were times when all the talking and gossiping got a bit tiring, even for her.

Louanne looked at Hannah and her mom. "How are you two doing this fine, beautiful morning?"

"Just fine, Louanne," Mrs. Crawford replied. "How about yourself? Do anything special last night?"

Louanne stuck the broom back in its spot, then turned around and grinned. "I sure did. Dwight picked me up and took me out for dinner and a movie in Chattanooga. He wanted to take me someplace where I could wear that new Anne Klein dress he bought me for Christmas. We had such a nice time. Did I tell y'all he got a new car?"

"Yes, you did," Grandma said as she brought a basket of clean towels up to the front desk and set them in front of Hannah to fold. "About seven times now. Maybe eight, I'm not quite sure. The color is blue, to match your beautiful blue eyes, is what you told us."

Louanne had been going out with Dwight for a couple of months now. She seemed to be head-over-heels with the guy and talked about him every chance she got. Hannah went to work folding towels while Louanne kept talking.

"Yes, that's right. Anyway, we went to a new restaurant last night. Have y'all heard of Chuck's Steak House? It was delicious, girls. A bit on the spendy side, but of course, I wasn't paying, so who cares, right?" She chuckled as she plopped down in her chair with an emery board and started filing one of her long fingernails. "Tonight we're having a nice evening in at my place. Can't decide what I should make to eat, though."

"How about spaghetti?" Hannah suggested as she folded another towel and added it to the pile. "I had supper with my friend Elsie last night and her mama's spaghetti was really good."

Louanne stopped filing and stared at Hannah. "Elsie Weston?"

"Yep," Hannah said. "We're in 4-H together."

Louanne got out of her chair and walked over to the reception desk. She narrowed her eyes. "Honey, where'd you get that sweater you got on? It looks like something you pulled out of your grandma's closet. You didn't do that, did you? It's really not very flattering on you."

Hannah looked down at the plain, purple sweater she had on. It was a little baggy, but so what? She liked it that way. It was comfortable. And maybe her black skirt was nothing special, but it wasn't like she was dressing for homecoming. She'd gone to church, for Pete's sake. As for where she got it, she couldn't remember, but it didn't matter anyway

66

because Louanne probably didn't want to know the answer to that question. She was just naturally critical of people, and it drove Hannah crazy.

"So tell me," Louanne said, leaning in, trying to seem sweet but looking more like a burglar eyeing a diamond necklace, "how are the Westons doing? Any news on their money problems?"

Hannah stood up and looked Louanne in the eye. "They're doing just fine. As for the rest of it, that's none of our business, and please don't ask me again." She picked up the folded towels and took them over to the shelf by the sinks.

"I'm just worried about them, that's all," Louanne said as she strolled back to her station. "Didn't mean nothing by it, I swear."

Hannah wanted to tell Louanne that Hannah knew she didn't care diddly-squat about the Westons, that she just liked to have stuff to gossip about with the ladies who came in to see her. But she bit her tongue and went back to the desk.

"Mama, can I take down all the Christmas decorations? I think it's about time, don't you?"

"You must have read my mind," Mrs. Crawford replied. "I was gonna ask you to do that today. Pretty soon it'll be time to think about Valentine's Day."

"Ooooh," Louanne squealed. "Valentine's Day! The most romantic day of the year. I can hardly wait to see what wonderful things Dwight will cook up for me."

Hannah couldn't help but think if Dwight knew what was good for him, he'd kick Louanne out of the kitchen and not cook up a single thing, but she didn't say a word.

"Anything in these little packages under this tree?" Hannah asked her mother.

"Nope. They're just for looks. Pack 'em up with the rest of the decorations and we'll use them again next year."

"Why, you hoping you'd find the horse of your dreams in one of them, Hannah?" Louanne teased. "Instead of that ugly old mule you ended up with?"

Hannah spun around and was about to tell her he wasn't ugly, and that she needed to stop saying such mean things, when the phone rang.

"Why don't you get that, Hannah?" Mrs. Crawford said before turning to Louanne. "I think my mother could use some help in the back, tallying up supplies. Could you please go check with her?"

Hannah took a deep breath, put a smile on her face, and picked up the phone. *Saved by the bell*, she thought. *Or ring. Whatever.*

Chapter 11

CONSTELLATION: Canis Minor
the Little Dog

*T*hat night, after supper, Hannah bundled up and went outside to bring Bart in for the night and give him his hay. It was clear and cold, so she'd put on a knit hat and gloves and her warmest coat. When she got to the pen, she stood there and watched Bart in the moonlight.

Louanne was wrong. He wasn't ugly. Not at all. Just like Elsie had said, he was different, but not in a bad way. Just . . . different. Bart turned his head and stared right at Hannah. And then, he walked toward her. He stopped, just inches away from the fence, and still he looked at her.

"Hey," she said. "How's it going out here? Kind of cold, isn't it?"

He blinked.

Hannah reached out and scratched his head between his

longish ears. As she continued to scratch, he moved his ears forward a bit and swished his tail a couple of times, clearly enjoying it.

"I'm sorry," she whispered. "I haven't been very nice to you. I mean, I haven't been terrible, but I haven't been nice either. I feel bad, and I want to make it up to you. I think I'm going to start by giving you a new name. Once I figure out what it is, of course."

"He likes you."

Hannah jumped a little, startled by the voice she hadn't expected to hear in the quiet of the night.

"I don't know about that," Hannah said as she gave Bart's muzzle a final pat, before she turned around to face her grandpa. He had his hands stuffed into his red-and-black-checkered wool coat. On his head, he wore the old straw cowboy hat he rarely took off.

"Did I ever tell you the story of Spot?" he asked Hannah.

"I don't think so."

He walked closer. "When I was a boy, we had a dog show up at our place one day. Just out of nowhere, there he was. No collar on him, but he looked well taken care of. Clean and well fed. We lived way out in the country, you know, and it seemed like we would have seen him before if he lived nearby. Still, we went around and asked everyone and no one knew anything about him. So Pop said we could keep him, but I really didn't want to keep him."

"How come?" Hannah asked.

"Because I tell you what, that dog was the ugliest thing you ever did see. Pop thought he might have been a cross between a Jack Russell and a Pomeranian, but it was just a guess. All I knew was that dog was one strange-looking animal. Someone in the family, I don't remember who, called him Spot one day and it stuck. As soon as that dog showed up, he was like one of the family. He'd follow any one of us around the farm, never straying far, and it was like he'd lived there his whole life."

"How old was he?"

"Hard to say. Grown, though, not a puppy, that's for sure. Shortly after we got him, we had a tragedy occur. My older brother, John, was killed in a hunting accident. We were all torn up about it, but my mother, it really knocked her for a loop. There were days she wouldn't get out of bed. But you know who stuck by her, never left her side, except to eat and go to the bathroom?"

"Spot?" Hannah said.

"That's right. He'd get up on the bed and lay with her, and we'd call and call and try to get him to come outside and do chores with us, but he'd have none of it. He wouldn't leave her side unless he absolutely had to."

Hannah's grandpa reached up and wiped at his face. *Was he crying*, she wondered? She'd never seen him cry. Since it was hard to see in the darkness, she couldn't know for sure.

"I bet she liked that," Hannah asked. "Spot sticking by her, I mean."

"Oh, yes. I remember, I peeked my head into her room one day and saw her stroking his little head. I think he helped her more than any of us could really understand. He may have been nothing special to look at, but that dog had a heart bigger than a lot of people I know, that's for sure."

He let those words hang in the darkness for a moment before he waved his hand at Bart and said, "Anyway, you want some help bringing him in?"

She shook her head. "No. I can do it. Thanks, though."

"You're welcome. Good night, sweetheart."

"Good night."

Grandpa turned back toward his house while Hannah went into the pen and led Bart to his stall in the barn like she'd been doing every night since New Year's Eve. After she fed him his hay, she gave him another pat and walked out into the quiet night.

As she made her way back to her house, she stopped and looked up at the sky. She found Orion's Belt again and thought about what Elsie had said, about stars and magic and being alive.

And that's when she decided to name the mule something magical. Something beautiful. He'd ended up here, with the Crawfords, through no fault of his, and maybe Hannah didn't understand why and maybe she'd been mad about it at first, but that didn't mean she had to stay mad.

"Good night, Stardust," Hannah whispered. "I hope you like your new name."

Chapter 12

Constellation: Cassiopeia
the Queen

"I'm sooooo happy to see you," Crystal said, throwing her arms around Hannah. "It feels like forever since I saw you last."

"Just two weeks, silly," Hannah said, as the girls turned and walked down the hallway toward their locker.

"Well, that's two weeks too long," Crystal said, looping her arm through her best friend's. Crystal looked amazing in a white-and-purple floral dress with a jean jacket over it, and her new blue cowboy boots to complete the look.

"I love them," Hannah said, pointing down. "Super cute. Is the dress new too?"

"Yes, ma'am," Crystal said. They stopped at their locker. "My grandma loves to shop, you know. She took us to the mall and we shopped the after-Christmas sales."

"Sounds fun," Hannah said as she worked on the combination. "I was hoping for some new clothes —"

"But Santa brought you a mule instead," Crystal teased. "Lucky you. Have you come up with any brilliant ideas as to how to get rid of him? The mule, I mean. Not Santa, obviously. Santa's a keeper, as long as he brings us cute boots."

Hannah opened the locker door and hung her backpack on one of the hooks inside. "His name is Stardust. Please don't call him 'the mule' anymore, all right? It sounds bad."

Crystal stuffed her backpack into the locker too, then spun around and put her hand on her hip. "I know, it does sound bad, because it *is* bad, and I'm so sorry you have to deal with this. You deserve better." She paused. "Wait. I thought his name was Bart."

Hannah shrugged and stuffed her hands in her jean pockets. "It was, but I changed it. Look, it's not as terrible as you make it sound." She remembered what Elsie had said. "He's just different, that's all. There's nothing wrong with being different, is there?"

"But a mule is kind of like a donkey, and donkeys are kind of . . ."

Before Crystal could finish her thought, Hannah spoke up. "A mule is half horse too you know."

Crystal didn't look impressed. Hannah threw her arms up in the air, exasperated. "It shouldn't even matter what he is! He's an animal who wants what all of us want."

"A cute pair of boots?"

Hannah shook her head, smiling. "No. To be loved. For who he is."

"So are you telling me you suddenly love him? Just a few days ago, you said —"

Hannah leaned up against the open locker door, her arms folded across her chest. "No, of course I don't love him. But I feel sorry for him." She groaned. "Oh, I don't know. I don't know what to think or how to feel. The whole situation is so messed up."

Before Crystal could respond, she heard the words "Hi, Hannah." She looked past Crystal to find Elsie standing there.

"Hey, Elsie," she replied. "You know Crystal, right?"

"Yeah. Hello."

"Hello," Crystal said. "We were just talking about you. Riding Bart. Er, I mean, Stardust."

Elsie's eyes got really big and her mouth opened in surprise. "You gave him a new name? Oh my gosh, Hannah, Stardust is beautiful. I love it!"

Hannah smiled. "Figured you would. Kind of have you to thank for it, with all of your talk about magic and stars the other night."

"Can you scoot over, please?" Crystal said, stepping forward. "I need to get my books."

"I better get going." Elsie gave a little wave. "I'll see you guys later."

"Bye," Hannah said. Crystal didn't say anything.

"Why do I get the feeling you don't like her very much?" Hannah asked.

"Because I don't," Crystal replied as she bent down, searching the bottom of their locker. "What happened to my pencil? I can't find it. Do you have an extra?"

Hannah grabbed her pencil case from her shelf. "But you don't even know her." She opened the case and got a pencil out. "She's a really nice girl. Just shy is all."

Crystal stood up and took the pencil out of Hannah's hand. "I just don't think she's my type."

This didn't make sense to Hannah. Not her type? "What does that even mean? You don't have to marry her, you know."

Crystal leaned in. "Have you heard about her family's money problems?"

Hannah held back a groan, and stared at Crystal. Not her too?

"Crystal, please don't be like that."

"Like what?"

"Like . . . the queen of small-town gossip. Louanne Dodger holds that title, and to be honest, I think the crown looks much better on her."

Before Crystal could respond, the bell rang, telling the girls they had five minutes to get to class. Hannah went to work gathering her books.

"Are you mad at me?" Crystal asked after Hannah slammed the door shut.

"No," Hannah said. She put her arm around Crystal. "But you shouldn't be so quick to judge. Elsie's a sweet girl. I promise."

"All right. I'll take your word for it."

"Please, don't just take my word for it. Get to know her. You'll see what I mean."

Crystal didn't say anything as they walked down the hallway. Hannah told herself Crystal was letting the advice sink in, even though she knew that probably wasn't it at all.

Chapter 13

Constellation: Leo
the Lion

On Wednesday, when Hannah got home from school, she found a letter from Mia waiting for her. She heated up some apple cider, grabbed a box of vanilla wafers, and went to her room to read the letter.

Dear Hannah,

Happy New Year! Did you have a fun winter break? What did you get for Christmas? You're not going to believe what I got. A karaoke machine! It's so much fun. My friends and I have been having a blast with it. My mom even gets in on it sometimes and belts out a tune.

They just announced the spring play at school, and Lacy Bell thinks I should try out. Caitlin had

SO MUCH FUN IN HER FALL PLAY, I'M KIND OF THINKING ABOUT DOING IT. THEY'RE DOING "THE SWORD IN THE STONE" AND THANKFULLY, IT'S NOT A MUSICAL. I MIGHT LIKE TO SING IN MY HOUSE WITH FRIENDS, BUT THERE'S NO WAY I WANT TO GET ON STAGE AND SING IN FRONT OF A WHOLE BUNCH OF STRANGERS. I HONESTLY DON'T KNOW HOW CAITLIN DOES IT!

ARE YOU HAVING FUN WEARING THE BRACELET? LIBBY TOLD ME IN A LETTER THAT SHE'D MAILED IT OFF FOR YOU TO WEAR. I WONDER IF WE'LL EACH GET A CHANCE TO WEAR IT AGAIN BEFORE CAMP STARTS UP AGAIN IN JULY. I'M SO EXCITED TO SEE WHAT CHARMS HAVE BEEN ADDED SINCE I LAST SAW IT.

I'M NOT REALLY A FAN OF JANUARY AND FEBRUARY. THEY'RE SO BORING. I JUST WANT JULY TO HURRY UP AND GET HERE SO I CAN SEE YOU, CAITLIN, AND LIBBY AGAIN. IT'S GOING TO BE SO AWESOME WHEN THE FOUR OF US ARE BACK TOGETHER AGAIN. I CAN'T WAIT!!

WRITE ME BACK WHEN YOU CAN, AND TELL ME ABOUT YOUR CHRISTMAS OR ANYTHING ELSE EXCITING THAT'S GOING ON. I MISS YOU!

YOUR CABIN 7 BFF,
MIA

Hannah set the letter down and let out a deep sigh. Of course Mia wanted to know what she got for Christmas. And Libby would probably want to know too. She knew she needed to write both of them and tell them, but not today. Her feelings about Stardust were too mixed up and she had no idea what to say about him. So for now, she just wouldn't say anything.

It was much easier that way.

Hannah had a Mane Attraction meeting that night. The club tried to alternate between educational meetings and riding meetings, where they got to spend time with real, live horses, and tonight was an educational one. Just like always, Mr. Crawford dropped Hannah off at the meeting and then went bowling for a couple of hours with some of his friends. When she walked in the room, a few minutes before seven, everyone looked at her and stopped talking.

"Hey, y'all," she said. "Am I interrupting something? Want me to step out so you can finish whatever it was you were discussing?"

Carson, tall and gangly, stood up and put his hands in his jeans pockets. He always wore plaid, button-down shirts and his black felt cowboy hat. On someone else, this look might have been cool, but on him, it looked like he was trying too hard.

"We were talking about you, actually," he said.

"Talking about how I'm sweeter than cotton candy?" Hannah asked, trying to be funny. "Sweeter than a piece of peach pie? Sweeter than sweet tea on a hot summer day?"

No one laughed. Hannah crossed her arms. "All right. I guess not. So tell me, what were you saying?"

Just then, Elsie walked in and stood next to Hannah. "What's going on?"

"Carson was just going to tell me what they were saying about me," Hannah explained. "Apparently Beauty by Design isn't the only place where gossip is king."

"We weren't gossiping," Darren said. "We were having a discussion."

"About what?" Elsie asked. "Tell us. We're part of the club too, you know."

"Sorry I'm late," Mr. Brody said as he rushed into the room carrying a cardboard box. "My mother called me, and while I love that woman dearly, it's hard to get her to stop talking sometimes."

When he got to the front of the room, he set the box

down and said, "What's going on? It's not like y'all to be so quiet."

"Nothing," Carson said, taking his seat.

"That's not true," Hannah said with a scowl. "They were discussing something before Elsie and I got here, and we want to know what it was."

"Is that so?" Mr. Brody said. "Well, by all means, please enlighten us. I'm curious too."

No one said anything for a moment. Then Darren spoke up. "We don't think Hannah should be in the club anymore. She's got a mule, not a horse. They're not the same thing."

"I kind of agree," said a girl named Rose. "When we ride in the Valentine's Day parade like we do every year, it's gonna look weird if she rides with us."

"Yep. They're right. She don't belong here," Carson said. "Not with a mule."

Hannah felt sick to her stomach. She couldn't believe what she was hearing. As she tried to think of how to respond, Elsie spoke up.

"She does *too* belong," Elsie said. "She belongs because she loves horses just like the rest of us. It's not like she got a lion or a tiger or a bear for Christmas. It's a mule, which is half horse, and which you can ride just like a horse. Stardust is just as good, if not better than a horse, trust me. I know because I rode him the other day."

"Why don't you two girls take a seat," Mr. Brody said. Hannah and Elsie did as he asked. "I agree with Elsie as far as the club goes," he went on. "Anyone is welcome, whether they own a horse or not. The only requirement, as we've said all along, is that members must have a love of horses."

"What about the parade?" Mary Beth asked. "Won't it look strange for the 4-H *horse* club to have a mule there?"

Hannah almost told the group that she didn't want to ride with them anyway. After all, she hadn't ridden Stardust by herself, let alone with a group. But she was curious as to what Mr. Brody had to say about it. Did he think Stardust should be allowed in the parade or not? She wanted him to say that it would be just fine for Hannah and Stardust to join the group. For once, she wanted to feel like it wasn't a big deal that she had a mule instead of a horse. If he'd just say that she could ride Stardust in the parade, then maybe she would stop feeling bad about the whole thing.

But that isn't what he said.

"I need to give the parade some thought," Mr. Brody said as he rubbed his chin. "Please understand, Hannah, this is nothing personal. It's just that whatever decision is made sets a precedent for the club. I may even need to consult with the regional 4-H advisor and see what she has to say about it." He looked directly at Hannah. "I'm sorry. I'll have a decision for you at our next meeting, all right?"

Hannah gave him a little nod. Although she and Elsie sat in the back of the room, and she could only see the backs of everyone's heads, she imagined all of them smirking with triumph.

"Okay," Mr. Brody said as he clapped his hands. "Time to start our meeting. I have a horse-judging video for you to watch, and after that, we'll play a trivia game. And of course, as always, we'll have treats and social time at the end. It's gonna be a fun evening!"

The way things had gone so far, Hannah wasn't so sure about that.

Chapter 14

Constellation: Lepus the Hare

Elsie pulled Hannah into a corner after they'd grabbed cupcakes at the end of the meeting. The other kids were gathered around someone's phone watching the latest and greatest video featuring an adorable rabbit. Mr. Brody was talking to a couple of the parents who had come to help for part of the meeting.

"I'm so sorry about what they were saying," Elsie said softly. "That wasn't nice. At all."

Hannah peeled the liner off of her chocolate caramel cupcake and set it on the small plate. "Well, *you* have nothing to be sorry for. Actually, I wanted to say thank you for sticking up for me. That was really sweet of you."

Elsie's eyes narrowed. "Mr. Brody better let you ride in the parade. I'll be furious if he says you can't."

"I'm not even sure I want to ride in the parade," Hannah said, tearing off a piece of the cupcake and eating it. "Mmmm, this is really good. Try it."

"Carson's mom made them," Elsie said before she took a bite and nodded in agreement.

"I hope he didn't poison mine," Hannah said. "I don't think he likes me very much."

"I don't think he likes anyone very much, except maybe himself," Elsie said. "And what do you mean you don't want to ride in the parade? Of course you do. You've got to show everyone how great Stardust is, in all the ways that are important."

"I still haven't ridden him yet," Hannah said, staring at her cupcake.

"Are you afraid?"

"Of Stardust?" Hannah asked. "I don't know what I am. Confused, I guess." She took another bite of her treat.

"You need to ride him. I swear, you won't be confused anymore after you ride him."

"Let's not talk about him anymore. How are things going for you?"

Elsie looked around and then leaned in. "Daddy said tonight at supper that we have to start packing soon. Our landlord is evicting us at the end of the month if we can't pay our rent."

So the rumors were true. Suddenly Hannah felt sick to her stomach again. "But where will you go?"

"I don't know," Elsie said. "Might have to move in with my grandparents for a while. And there isn't much room at their place, so it doesn't sound fun at all."

"Where do they live?"

"Houston, Texas." Elsie took Hannah's empty plate from her and threw them in the trash.

When she returned, Hannah said, "Elsie, I'm so sorry. I feel terrible for you and your family. Is there anything we can do?"

"I don't think so. I mean, unless you know someone who's hiring. My daddy's smart and a hard worker, he just needs someone to give him a chance."

"I'm gonna talk to my dad and see if he knows of any jobs," Hannah told Elsie.

"Thanks for wanting to help. It's real nice of you."

Nervously, Hannah fingered the charm bracelet as she tried to think of more ways to help. Then, she had an idea. "Here," she said, unclasping the bracelet from her wrist. "Take this and wear it. It might bring you luck."

Elsie gave her a quizzical look as she took the bracelet from Hannah. "Luck? What do you mean?"

Hannah wasn't sure how much she should tell her. She wasn't even sure if the bracelet was actually lucky or, if it was, if it would work on someone outside of the four camp friends who bought it. "Just put it on," Hannah suggested. "See if anything happens."

Still looking confused, Elsie put the bracelet on her wrist. Hannah waited a few seconds and asked, "Did you see anything?"

"See anything? Besides you standing here next to me?"

"Yeah. Like, in your mind, did anything pop up?"

"No. Hannah, I'm kind of worried about you. Do you need to sit down?"

Hannah smiled. "Sorry, I know it sounds strange. Never mind. Please, just wear it. If it really is lucky, you can use all the luck you can get right now."

Elsie fingered the three charms: the flower, the bird, and the peppermint candy. "It's really cute. Where'd you get it?"

"I bought it along with my three best friends from camp, while we were on a field trip together. We're taking turns wearing it."

"Oh, that's sweet," Elsie said, before the corners of her mouth turned down. "But won't your friends be upset that you let me borrow it?"

Hannah shrugged. "We didn't really talk about loaning it to other people. I'm pretty sure they won't mind. Like I said, you need all the luck you can get right now."

"If you say so. I'll get it back to you soon, okay?"

"I'm not worried," Hannah said. At least, not about getting the bracelet back. But as far as Elsie's family getting kicked out of their house?

She was *very* worried about that.

Chapter 15

Constellation: Columba
the Dove

The next evening, Hannah decided to ask her dad about job openings, like she'd told Elsie she would do.

"Daddy," she said as she ate the last bite of her cheeseburger casserole. "Are they hiring at the electric company?"

"Not right now, sweetheart."

"Why are you asking?" Eric said. "Aren't you a little young to be looking for work?"

"I'm not asking for me. It's for Elsie's dad. If he doesn't find something soon and pay their rent, the entire family is going to get evicted."

"It's a sad situation, that's for sure," Mrs. Crawford said before she took a sip of water. "Wish there was something we could do to help, but at this point, I think it's going to take a big, fat miracle."

"If that happens, I'm writing a book about it," Adam said.

"And I'll direct the movie," Eric said. "Everyone loves those miracle stories."

Hannah ignored her brothers. "There must be something we could do. What if we made them a bunch of meals, so they could use their grocery money for rent instead?"

"Oh, honey," her mother said. "It wouldn't be nearly enough. I know it's hard to sit back and feel helpless, but sometimes all we can do is just be a good friend."

"That's right," her father said. "Be a good listener for Elsie. Let her cry on your shoulder if she needs to. And when you can, try to make her laugh. Because you know what I say."

Hannah sighed. "I know, I know. Laughter is the best medicine. But none of that will fix their problem."

Her mother stood up. "I don't like seeing you so worried about this. Tell you what. We'll leave the boys to clean up and do the dishes, while you and I go visiting this evening. Someone else we know is in need of a friend."

"Who's that?" Hannah asked.

"It's a surprise. Now, do me a favor and go wrap up some of those chocolate chip cookies you made after school. I know she'll appreciate some of those."

*   *   *

Hannah decided her mother needed someone to sit down and explain what a surprise is supposed to be. Or what it's *not* supposed to be. For example, a surprise Christmas gift is not supposed to be a mule instead of a horse. And a surprise visit is not supposed to be to see Louanne Dodger.

When Louanne opened the front door of her apartment, with her mascara smudged so much around her eyes that she looked like a raccoon, Hannah glared at her mother. Mrs. Crawford didn't skip a beat though.

"Sweetie, we stopped by to make sure you're doing all right." She held out the plate of cookies. "Hannah baked these earlier today and we thought they might cheer you up. Chocolate is a girl's best friend and all of that."

As Louanne took the cookies, Hannah said, "I think the saying is about diamonds, Mama. Diamonds are a girl's best friend."

Louanne's bottom lip began to tremble. "And I'll never get a diamond from Dwight now," she said with a shaky voice, before she closed her eyes and started to cry.

"Oh, dear," Mrs. Crawford said, stepping forward and putting her arm around Louanne. "It's going to be okay.

93

You'll see." She led Louanne inside and motioned to Hannah to close the door.

Mrs. Crawford took the plate of cookies and set them on a coffee table that sat in front of a blue-and-green plaid sofa. While she and Louanne settled in on the sofa, Hannah stood there, looking around. There was a curio cabinet in the corner filled with music boxes. Hannah was pretty sure she'd never seen so many music boxes. On the walls were pictures of various country music singers, holding guitars or sitting at the piano. Louanne was crazy about music, that was for sure.

Hannah sat down in a wooden rocking chair across from the sofa while her mother fished a tissue out of her purse for Louanne. She wished she could be anywhere but here, because this was not fun. Not even remotely fun. Like, scrubbing the toilet would have been more fun than sitting there, watching Louanne cry her eyes out.

"I'm sorry," Louanne said after she blew her nose. "My heart is just completely and utterly broken, you know?"

"Well, what happened?" Mrs. Crawford asked. "I thought the two of you were getting along like two doves in a tree."

"That's just it," Louanne said, leaning back into the sofa. "We were. And then he came over here last night and told me it was over. When I asked him why, all he said was, 'sometimes feelings are too complicated to put into words.'"

"I agree with that, actually," Hannah said, thinking about her feelings for Stardust.

Mrs. Crawford gave her daughter a look that told Hannah that probably wasn't the best thing to say right now.

Louanne wiped her nose again. "He said I just had to trust him that this was for the best. That we both deserved better." She shook her head. "It doesn't make any sense to me. We had the best time together."

As Louanne looked at Mrs. Crawford, tears filled her eyes again. Mrs. Crawford pulled her close and stroked Louanne's hair. "Shhhh. There, there. I know it hurts. I wish there was something I could do for you, honey, but it's just gonna have to hurt for a while. There's no real cure for heartbreak except time. Sometimes, lots of it."

That's when Hannah figured out why her mother had brought her along. To show her that being a friend didn't always mean fixing things, because sometimes, it was simply impossible. It meant listening and being there, just like she and her daddy had said earlier.

Hannah stood up. "Mama, I thought I might make us some tea, if that's all right?" Her grandma had taught her that when you don't know what else to do, offer to do that, because a warm cup of tea is always appreciated.

"That's a fine idea," her mother replied.

"Tea bags are in the canister, next to the toaster," Louanne said in between sniffles. "I stocked up when Dwight told me he preferred tea over coffee."

She burst into tears again. Hannah scurried off to the kitchen, glad to have something to do besides sit there and feel helpless.

It seemed like she felt helpless a lot recently, Hannah realized. And she didn't like it one bit.

Chapter 16

Constellation: Capricornus the Goat

On Friday, the science teachers passed out forms for the science fair that would take place in April. They also shared a list of possible experiments, with a link to a website that had even more ideas. There were a few on the list involving astronomy, and one that sounded especially interesting to Hannah. After school, she found Elsie at her locker to see what she thought of the experiment.

Elsie had on a short brown skirt and a soft pink sweater with brown trim that Hannah had never seen before.

"I love your outfit," Hannah told her. "Is it new?"

"Thanks," Elsie said. "I got it for Christmas. I couldn't wear it, though, because we had to return it and get a different size. My mom isn't very good at keeping track of our sizes. Since there's so many of us, you know?"

"Well, I'm glad you got something nice, even though your family is kind of struggling right now," Hannah said.

"Me too," Elsie said. "It helps that my mother is a thrifty shopper. You should see the number of coupons she clips every week for groceries. It's pretty amazing. Anyway, did you need something?"

Hannah smiled. "I was wondering, do you want to work together on a project for the science fair? There's this cool one that involves tracking the changes of the moon to see if it makes a difference on how well you can see the stars. It'd be pretty fun doing it together, right?"

Elsie put on her coat, grabbed her backpack, and shut her locker door. "That does sound fun," she said with absolutely no enthusiasm. "Except I don't think I can say yes, because I probably won't be here in April. You should find someone else to do it with you."

"Maybe we could work on it together until you know for sure if you're moving or not," Hannah suggested. "I could finish it on my own if I had to." She paused. "It'll be way more fun doing it with you, is all."

"I don't know," Elsie said softly. "Can I think about it and let you know? The forms aren't due for a while yet, right?"

She looked so sad, and it made Hannah feel terrible. She hadn't meant to stir up Elsie's worries all over again.

Thinking about what her mother had said, Hannah decided that the only thing she could do was to be a good friend. "Sure. That's fine. Hey, do you want to come over tomorrow? We can do whatever you want to do. Watch a movie or make cookies again. Something that will cheer you up."

"Can I ride Stardust?" Elsie asked.

Hannah shrugged. "I guess so."

"Will you ride him too?" she asked.

"I don't know about that."

"Please? Pretty please? It'd cheer me up for sure."

Hannah bit her lip. How could she possibly say no when she put it like that? "You drive a hard bargain, as my daddy says. All right. I'll do it."

"Yippee!" Elsie said as she threw her arm around Hannah and gave her half-a-hug.

That night, it was Hannah's turn to do the dishes and clean up the kitchen. Her mother offered to help her.

"Louanne made it in to work today," Mrs. Crawford said as she wiped down the stove. "She seemed a little better. Said she really appreciated us coming over there last night."

Hannah set a bowl in the dishwasher and turned around to face her mother. "I promise you, I will never go on and on like that over some guy. It was worse than a lost baby goat crying for its mama."

Her mother laughed. "Now, now. Never say never. You don't know what the future might bring. Though a mother always hopes her kids won't have to endure any kind of heartbreak, I think in life, with its ups and downs, it's pretty much inevitable."

"Inevitable?" Hannah asked. "What's that mean?"

"Means you can't avoid it."

"Maybe not, but Mama, she cried when she thought of how much Dwight loves tea. It was ridiculous." Hannah went back to the pile of dishes.

"Well, we did a good thing, anyway. She needed a little cheering up, that's for sure."

"Speaking of cheering up, I invited Elsie to come over tomorrow," Hannah said after she rinsed off a plate. "She wants to ride Stardust again."

"Wonderful. That'll be good for her. Get her mind off their problems for a while."

"Yeah, that's what I thought." Hannah paused. "I told her I'd ride Stardust too."

She felt her mother's arm around her shoulders. "I'm happy to hear that. It's time you gave him a try. He needs to be ridden, sweetie. It's not good for him to stand around, day after day, doing nothing."

"Daddy said he's been riding him sometimes," Hannah said, grabbing a bunch of silverware and putting it in the dishwasher. "So it's not like he's doing absolutely nothing."

"Yes, but your father doesn't want to have to do that forever. Hannah, we bought him for you."

Didn't her mother know this was not new information? Hannah squeezed her mouth shut so she wouldn't say anything she might regret. Her family simply didn't understand how hard it was to be the weird kid in the horse club. The one who had to get special permission to ride in the Valentine's Day parade.

What was so wrong about wanting to be a normal girl with a normal horse, like everyone else?

"You've got to give him a chance," her mother continued.

Hannah sighed. "I know it may not seem like it, but I'm trying, Mama. I really am."

"I believe you," she replied. "You're a good person, Hannah Nicole Crawford. And that animal out there is a good mule. I just want things to work out between the two of you. That's all."

Chapter 17

Constellation: Taurus the Bull

Crystal called later that night. "Hey, my mom told me about this fun cake decorating class happening tomorrow afternoon at Craft World. She invited me to go with her, and I'm like, I have to see if Hannah can go too. She's the one who likes to bake, after all. And we haven't done anything fun together in forever."

"Tomorrow?" Hannah gulped. "As in, the Saturday that is the day after today?"

"That would be correct. Please don't tell me you have plans. Please? Don't you know your life will not be complete until you've learned how to make roses out of frosting?"

"I have plans," Hannah said, leaning back against her headboard. She closed the textbook that sat in her lap. "Sorry."

"What kind of plans?"

"Well, I invited Elsie to come over. She wants to ride Stardust again."

"Oh. Well, call her and reschedule. She'll understand, right? Hannah, think about it. Cake and frosting, two of the best things in the entire world."

"It sounds really fun, but I can't reschedule. That'd be rude. What am I supposed to say, sorry, something better came up?"

"Yes. I think that is exactly what you should tell her. I mean, it's true, right?"

Hannah didn't like where this was headed. "You really don't like her, do you? I wish you'd just give her a . . ."

She stopped as she realized what she was about to say. The same thing her mama had just said about Stardust. How could she be mad at her best friend for being that way with Elsie when Hannah was doing the same kind of thing when it came to the mule?

"Hannah?" Crystal said. "You there?"

"Yeah," she said. "I'm here, but I gotta go. Sorry I can't decorate cakes with you. I'll see you at school on Monday. Bye."

Before Crystal could protest, Hannah ended the call and put her face in her hands. She was treating Stardust *exactly* the same way Crystal treated Elsie.

Crystal wasn't really mean to Elsie, of course. But she wasn't nice either. And why? Because her family was having money problems? What did that have to do with the kind of person Elsie was or the kind of friend she might be to Crystal?

Crystal was judging Elsie on things Elsie had no control over in the same way Hannah was judging Stardust. Hannah felt sick to her stomach at the realization, and she knew there was only one thing to do.

She needed to give Stardust a fair chance.

When Hannah opened the door to let Elsie in on Saturday, she was greeted with a big smile on Elsie's face.

"Hi!" Hannah said. "Come on in. You look happy. Excited to ride Stardust?"

"Yes, I am," Elsie said as she stepped inside, "but that's not why I can't stop smiling. My daddy has a job interview next week. At a really good company." She paused as her smile slipped away. "Oh no. I hope I'm not jinxing it by telling you."

"Are you still wearing the lucky bracelet?" Hannah asked as she shut the door and led Elsie into the family room.

Elsie pushed the sleeve of her jacket up. "Yep. Haven't taken it off since you gave it to me."

"Well, hopefully it will do its thing and your daddy will get that job. I'm so happy for you guys!"

"Yeah. Me too. He said they sounded really excited to meet with him when they called him yesterday afternoon."

"I don't even know what he does," Hannah said, taking a seat on the sofa. "I probably should have asked you. Although the electric company doesn't have openings of any kind right now, in case you were wondering. I checked like I said I would."

"Thanks," Elsie said, taking a seat in the overstuffed chair next to the sofa. "I'm not really sure what he does either, to be honest. Management or something like that. He likes working with people, I guess." She rubbed her hands together. "Okay, enough about that. You ready to get on Stardust for the very first time?"

"Yep. I think I am. Daddy's out in the barn now, saddling him up for us."

"I am so glad you're doing this, Hannah. It's going to be great. Just wait and see. You're not nervous, are you?"

"Yeah. A little bit. I hope he isn't mad at me. I haven't been very fair to him, you know?"

Elsie smiled. "He's not gonna be mad at you. He's going to be like Taurus the bull, I just know it."

"What do you mean?"

"I was reading about Taurus in one of my constellation books last night. The ruler of the gods, Jupiter, took on the shape of a bull when he became enchanted with Europa, who was the princess of . . . something. I can't remember exactly. Anyway, when the princess saw the bull, she loved his beauty and gentleness, and they played together on the beach. Eventually, she climbed onto his back and they swam out to sea together."

"Oh, wow," Hannah said. "That's beautiful. What happened to them? Did she ever find out who he really was?"

"Yes," Elsie said. "He took her to a special place and revealed who he really was. I think we are supposed to imagine they lived happily ever after."

Hannah stood up. "So, are you saying Stardust isn't a mule at all, but some mythological ruler of gods?"

Elsie laughed. "No, silly. I'm trying to tell you he loves you and the two of you are going to live happily ever after."

"I don't know about that," Hannah said. "But let me get my boots on so I can finally ride him. I think that's the first step toward happily ever after."

Chapter 18

Constellation: Draco the Dragon

It was cold outside. Too cold for a cowboy hat, Hannah decided. She put on a knit hat and some gloves and loaned Elsie some too, since she hadn't thought to bring any. As they walked toward the barn, the dirt hard and crunchy beneath their feet and the country air fresh and crisp, Hannah felt butterflies swarming around in her stomach.

"Afternoon, ladies," Mr. Crawford said as the girls reached him and Stardust, standing inside the barn. "Nice day for a ride, isn't it?"

"It's cold," Hannah said. "I think it'll be a quick one."

"Nah, it's not so bad," he said. "All right, who's first?"

"You should go," Elsie said, giving Hannah a gentle nudge with her elbow.

"I don't know."

"It'll be fine," her daddy said. "You'll see. You want some help getting on him?"

Hannah had ridden horses before. That's why the Mane Attraction 4-H club was so great. At the riding meetings, everyone got to ride, whether they had their own horse or not. Still, she was nervous, and she didn't want to do the wrong thing.

"Yes, please," she said to her father as she stroked Stardust's neck. Last night, after she'd fed him, she'd spent some time brushing him and talking to him. His coat looked nice and shiny in the daylight.

Mr. Crawford gave Hannah a boost up, and just like that, she was settling into the saddle. He slipped the reins he'd been holding over Stardust's head and handed them to her.

"He knows the way to the corral by now," Mr. Crawford said. "When you're ready, loosen the reins and give him a little squeeze with your boots."

"You look awesome up there," Elsie said, silently clapping her gloved hands together. "You really do. I wish I had a smartphone, I'd take a picture."

Mr. Crawford reached into the pocket of his lined jean jacket and pulled out his phone. "Here. Use mine."

Hannah's heart was beating fast in her chest. It wasn't because she was afraid though. She was excited. Really excited.

"All right, Stardust. Giddy up." She sat forward in her seat and squeezed her legs and just like that, he started moving.

As they approached the corral, Mr. Crawford ran ahead and opened the gate. Stardust's ears were forward and alert, but he didn't seem to be nervous about any of it. He strolled right in and Hannah heard the gate click shut behind them.

They rode around the arena, and Hannah could hardly believe what a nice, steady ride he was. There wasn't a lot of swaying from side-to-side like she'd experienced on a horse. She was curious as to why that was, but for now, she decided to just sit back and enjoy it.

After a few times around, she decided to do as Elsie had done last weekend and move him into a trot. He picked up speed at her command, and Hannah smiled. She loved going faster, the cold wind pricking her face, making her eyes water. Around and around they went and she was so comfortable, she wondered why it'd taken her so long to do this.

She loved riding. Always had. She remembered the first time, at the age of five, like it was yesterday, on the old horse named Pearl that her grandparents used to have. Pearl died a year later, and since then, all she'd wanted was a horse to call her own so she could ride whenever she felt like it.

When Hannah finally brought the mule to a stop, she looked over at her father and Elsie, who stood outside the corral. They could not have looked happier if she'd been riding a unicorn.

Hannah swung her leg around Stardust and jumped off him, like she'd been riding him forever. "Oh my gosh, that was so fun," she said, her cheeks tingly from the cold. She gave Stardust a few pats and looked into his left eye. "Thank you," she whispered to him, before she looked over at Elsie and her father. "I cannot believe what a smooth ride he is."

"I told you so," Elsie said. "Didn't I tell you that?" She did a little happy dance. "I'm so glad you finally rode him, Hannah!"

Mr. Crawford walked over and gave his daughter a big hug. "I'm so proud of you, honey. And of Stardust too. You gave him a chance and he delivered for you."

"You need to thank Elsie," Hannah told him. "She's the one who finally got me to ride him."

"Well, thank you kindly, then," he told Elsie. "Shall we call you the miracle worker from now on?"

Elsie shook her head. "No, that's okay. It wasn't *that* hard. It's not like I was trying to convince her to ride a dragon or something."

Hannah laughed. "That wouldn't take much convincing either. That'd be cool! Okay, your turn to ride Stardust, Els. He's all warmed up for you."

"Are you sure you're not too cold? I mean, we can go inside and bake cookies if you'd rather do that."

"I'm fine!" Hannah replied. "I want you to ride him. And then I might ride him again. Because, honestly, I can't wait to ride him again!"

Mr. Crawford laughed and then said to Elsie, "I think you've created a monster."

Chapter 19

Constellation: Pyxis the Compass

Again on Sunday, and every day after school, Hannah rode Stardust. The cold snap continued, but it didn't stop her. She just bundled up and went out anyway. Stardust would see her coming and walk to greet her at the fence of the pen. Hannah's grandpa was usually home and helped her get him ready to ride.

On Thursday, after she changed and put on extra layers of clothes, she ran out to the pen. Except this time, her heart skipped a beat when she didn't find him there.

"Stardust?" she called, walking toward the barn.

"We're in here," she heard her grandpa call from inside.

Hannah smiled. Her grandpa must have come out early to get him ready for her. She needed to tell him that after helping with the saddle and bridle all week, she felt like she could do it by herself now.

Except, when she went into the barn, she didn't find Stardust ready to ride. Instead she found her grandpa kneeling down, with Stardust's leg bent up and resting on her grandpa's knee.

"What are you doing?" Hannah asked, making sure to stay back so she didn't startle Stardust while her grandpa worked on him.

"I noticed he was limping real bad. Seems he stepped on a sharp rock that caused a small hole near the outer edge of his hoof, and a tiny pebble got embedded in the hole." He gently pushed the mule's leg away and let it drop to the ground as he stood up.

"Is he going to be okay?" Hannah asked.

"Yes, I got the pebble out, so he should be fine," her grandpa said, patting Stardust's side as he walked around to where Hannah stood. "But I need to call the vet and find out what we need to do next. I suspect we soak it in something. Maybe Epsom salts. And I might need to bandage it so nothing else gets in there. I'm afraid riding him is out of the question for a week or so, though, as it heals up."

"Right," Hannah said. "I wouldn't want to make it any worse." She glanced over at Stardust, wondering if he was in pain. "I feel so bad for him. Can I brush him?"

Grandpa patted her shoulder. "Of course you can. I'm

gonna go inside and give the vet a call. Figure out what we do next."

"You sure it's not that serious?"

Her grandpa smiled. "It shouldn't be, as long as we do the right thing and take good care of him. He'll be fine, Hannah. Try not to worry."

"Okay."

"I guess the good news is you've become attached to the fella, huh?" He put his hands in his coat pockets. "We're all real happy to see the two of you getting along so well. He's a wonderful animal."

"Yes. He is. Thanks for taking care of him, Grandpa."

"You're welcome. I'll see you in a bit."

After he left, Hannah talked to Stardust as she went to the shelf where his brush was kept. "I'm sorry about your hoof. I know it probably hurts, but Grandpa will get you fixed up in no time."

She went to his head and stroked his cheek. Stardust lowered his head so his big brown eyes looked at her. "You don't look very happy," she told him. "Trust me, I feel the same way."

Hannah brushed his neck and was working her way down his chest when her phone buzzed.

"Sorry, bud," she said as she stepped back and fished the

phone out of her pocket. She set the brush down on the ground so she'd have her hands free.

"Hello?"

"Hi, Hannah?"

"Yeah?"

"It's Elsie," she said.

"Oh, hey."

"I didn't have your cell phone number since I don't have one myself, but I called the house phone and one of your brothers picked up. He said you were outside and I could call you at this number."

"What's up?" Hannah asked. "Everything okay?"

"Um, not exactly." She paused. "Look, I have really bad news, and I've kept it from you for days, and my mama said it was time to finally come clean about it. You know, tell you about the thing I really don't want to tell you."

"Oh no. Do you have to move to Houston?"

"Oh, I'm not sure about that yet. Like I told you at school, the interview went well. We're just waiting to hear back. What I need to tell you is . . . I'm so sorry, but I've lost your charm bracelet."

Hannah blinked a few times as she tried to process Elsie's words. "Lost it? What do you mean?"

"I mean, on Sunday, I noticed it was gone. I hadn't taken it off; it just fell off, I guess. Somehow. I don't know, Hannah. I've looked so hard for it. Every day, I've looked, in every single place I could think of." She started to cry. "I'm afraid it's gone."

"No, no, no," Hannah said, reeling backward until she leaned up against the wall of one of the stalls. "It can't be gone. It's *not* gone, Elsie. It's lost, which means it's somewhere, waiting to be found. Don't you understand? Caitlin, Mia, and Libby, the four of us from camp, we're charm sisters. It's our lucky bracelet, and I *have* to find it."

Elsie sniffled. "I've looked everywhere, Hannah. I'm so sorry, but I think you have to tell them. You have to tell them that I lost it."

Chapter 20

CONSTELLATION: Lacerta
the Lizard

*H*annah didn't sleep very well Thursday night. She was worried about Stardust, even if her grandpa said he'd be okay. And of course, she was worried about the bracelet. What would her camp friends say if she had to tell them it was gone forever? She tried to imagine avoiding the three of them for the next six months by not writing to them and then showing up at camp without the bracelet. They'd hate her for sure. Wouldn't they?

On Friday, Hannah was tired and grouchy. She did her best to avoid talking to anyone until lunchtime. But as she headed to the cafeteria, she knew this was her chance to pick Elsie's brain and help her figure out where else to look for the charm bracelet. Crystal was waiting for Hannah in their usual meeting spot, next to the vending machine that sold bottled water and juices.

"I'm sorry, I'm going to eat with Elsie today," Hannah explained. "I really need to talk to her. It's important."

"Okay," Crystal said, like she understood, even if she didn't understand what was going on, exactly. "See ya later."

Hannah looked around the cafeteria and spotted Elsie in the hot lunch line. "Can we talk?" Hannah asked her. "I brought my lunch, so I can go grab us a table way in the back."

"Okay," Elsie said softly. Hannah noticed she looked pale, with dark rings under her eyes. If Hannah hadn't slept well last night, Elsie probably hadn't slept well since she'd noticed the bracelet had gone missing.

When Elsie sat down across from her, Hannah put down her sandwich and was about to drill her on how it could have happened, when she looked into Elsie's eyes. She looked *so* sad. Sadder than a kid who'd lost his mother in the grocery store. Sadder than a lizard in the rain. Sadder than a birth-day cake without candles.

Hannah decided that before she did anything else, she needed to try to make Elsie feel better. As hard as it might be to do that, she knew it was the right thing to do.

"I'm so sorry," Elsie said, before Hannah could speak. "I mean, I know it doesn't get your bracelet back, but I want you to know, I feel really bad."

"I know," Hannah replied. "I can tell. You look like you haven't slept in a week."

Elsie poked a French fry with her fork and avoided Hannah's eyes. "I haven't, to be honest. Thanks to my daddy's interview and the lost bracelet, I'm a knot of worries, as my mama likes to say."

"Please, try not to feel bad, okay? Whatever happens, it'll be fine. I'll be fine. I wish you'd told me sooner. I feel terrible that you've been carrying around that worry all by yourself."

"I just kept hoping I'd find it. I mean, you don't know how hard I've looked for it."

Hannah popped a green grape into her mouth and pushed the baggie toward Elsie, encouraging her to take one too. Elsie complied.

"So, when do you remember seeing it last?" Hannah asked.

Elsie shook her head. "I'm not sure. I didn't notice it was gone until Sunday evening, when it was my turn to shower."

"What do you mean, your turn?" Hannah asked.

Elsie's cheeks turned pink as she nibbled on a fry. "It probably sounds strange, but since there's so many of us, we have assigned days for showers. My mom is kind of obsessed about keeping all of us on a schedule. Not just for showers, but laundry and other chores too."

Hannah nodded. "Oh, right. I guess it would suck to want to take a shower before school and have a line of four people ahead of you."

Elsie smiled. "Exactly. Anyway, back to the bracelet. It's frustrating because the only time I actually remember seeing it was when I showed it to you on Saturday. But it's been cold and I've been wearing long sleeves. I figure it could have fallen off any time between Saturday afternoon and Sunday night."

Hannah took a bite of her sandwich as she thought about that. "So what did you do on Sunday?"

"Got up and helped my mom with breakfast. We made French toast. Both of us looked in every drawer and cupboard in that kitchen."

"Okay, so what'd you do after that?"

"Got dressed and went to church." Elsie's eyes grew wide. "Oh no! I didn't check at church. Hannah, I can't believe I didn't think of that. We were home most of the day on Sunday, so I kept thinking it had to be in the house. But maybe it fell off while we were at church."

"Or even on your way there, you know? You should check the car."

Elsie sat back, a look of relief on her face. "Yeah. That's a good idea. I'll check our van when we get home. If it's not there, I'll ask one of my parents to take me to church on Saturday to look for it."

"Do you want me to go with you?" Hannah asked.

"No, you don't have to do that," Elsie said. "I can ask my brothers and sisters to go and help me. You should spend your weekend riding Stardust, now that you know how much you love doing that."

"Actually, I can't," Hannah said, before she ate some more grapes.

"How come?"

She told Elsie about his hoof and how they'd had to soak it in Epsom salts and then how her grandpa had taken some bandages and duct tape and made a bootie for him to wear.

"Is he going to be all right?" Elsie asked. "I mean, it's not serious, is it?"

"Grandpa says as long as he cleans it a couple of times a day and we keep it bandaged so it can heal, he'll be fine."

"I'm sorry to add to your worries," Elsie said, picking up her hamburger. "But hopefully we'll find the bracelet this weekend, and you won't have that to worry about anymore."

Hannah went back to eating her sandwich. She didn't want to tell Elsie what she was really thinking.

What if someone found the bracelet and took it home?

Friday night, Mrs. Crawford insisted Hannah go to the beauty shop the following day. She said it wouldn't do any good for Hannah to mope around about Stardust and the lost bracelet.

Elsie had told Hannah she'd call her as soon as they got back from the church. She hadn't found it in the van, which is what Hannah had been hoping for. To Hannah, it seemed like the chances of finding it in such a public place were close to zero. Her mother, however, felt differently. She believed if someone at church found it, that person would do the right thing and turn it in to the office.

If only Hannah had the charm bracelet to help bring a little bit of luck into the awful situation, she thought, as they drove to the beauty shop on Saturday. All she could do was cross her fingers and hope for the best.

The three of them were the first ones to arrive, so Hannah went in the back room and got to work folding towels. Louanne and the receptionist, Martha, arrived a few minutes later. Hannah knew this because she could hear the two of them chatting away up front. A few minutes later, Louanne appeared, looking like she'd seen a ghost. She huddled up against the wall, next to the doorway, trying to stay out of sight.

"What's wrong?" Hannah asked.

"Oh, Hannah, I can't do it. I just can't."

Hannah set the towel she'd been folding down and went over to where Louanne stood. "What do you mean? Do what?"

"There's a woman out there I've never seen before. She's my first appointment and she's . . ." Louanne wrinkled her face up.

"She's what?"

Louanne leaned in toward Hannah and whispered. "Repulsive. She's got burns on her face or something. I'm not exactly sure. Can you go and tell your grandma I've come down with a stomach bug? That I need to go on home? Maybe she or your mother can fit her in."

Hannah had had just about enough of Louanne and her judgmental ways. After all the stuff that had happened the previous week, Hannah just couldn't take one more frustrating thing. She just couldn't.

So Hannah smiled sweetly and said, "No, I will not do that. I would never do that. That woman deserves a nice haircut like anybody else. Can't you please stop being like this?"

"Being like what?" Louanne asked, looking positively shocked at the way Hannah was speaking to her.

"Acting like Miss High and Mighty because you've got a prettier face than most folks," Hannah said, crossing her arms over her chest. "Maybe I was a bit like you at first when it came to Stardust, but I've learned my lesson. You really and truly can't judge a book by its cover. So please, go cut that woman's hair, and be nice to her!"

Louanne stood there, speechless.

A moment later, Mrs. Crawford appeared. "Louanne? You do know you're keeping your client, Susan, waiting, right?"

Louanne picked up a couple of towels from the pile. "Sorry. I'm coming."

Once Hannah was alone again, she did a fist pump in the air. After all, it felt good to have something finally go her way.

Chapter 21

Constellation: Sagitta
the Arrow

Louanne did an amazing job on Susan's hair. She had thick brown hair that just needed someone to put a style to it. Louanne shaped it into a long bob and it looked really nice. Everyone in the salon told Susan it looked wonderful, and she left with a smile on her face.

In the car later, Mrs. Crawford asked Hannah if there was anything she and Grandma should know about the conversation she'd been having in the back room with Louanne. Despite the feelings Hannah had toward Louanne's sometimes-obnoxious behavior, Hannah didn't want to get Louanne in trouble. After all, in the end, Louanne had done the right thing.

"She was a bit nervous about talking to the new client today," Hannah said.

"Because of the burns on her face?" her grandma asked.

"Yes," Hannah said.

"What'd you tell her?" Mrs. Crawford asked, turning around and looking at Hannah in the backseat.

Hannah shrugged and looked out the window, trying not to make a big deal out of it. "I don't really remember. I think I said something about Stardust teaching me you can't judge a book by its cover."

"That was a good thing to say," her grandma replied. "And completely, one hundred percent true."

"Are you planning to ride Stardust in the Valentine's Day parade, then?" Mrs. Crawford asked.

"I don't know," Hannah said. "That's up to the 4-H leaders. At first I didn't care whether I did or not, but now, I'll be upset if they tell me I can't ride him."

"You've dreamed about it forever, it seems," Mrs. Crawford said. "I hope they do the right thing."

"I hope so too," Hannah said as she reached for the charm bracelet out of habit. Without the lucky bracelet to help her, though, she wasn't feeling very confident.

When they got home, Hannah found a letter from Libby waiting for her. Instead of getting happy and excited when she saw the envelope, dread filled her. She didn't open it. In fact, she took it to her room and stuffed it into her top desk drawer.

Elsie hadn't called yet, and Hannah wondered why. She decided she couldn't wait any longer to hear from her. She dialed her number. It rang once, twice, then three times before someone answered.

"Hello?" a little voice said.

"Hi. Who's this?"

"This is Minnie."

"Oh, hi, Minnie. This is Hannah, Elsie's friend? Is she home?"

"Yes. She's in her room. She was sad when we didn't find your bracelet at church. So she came home and said she wanted to be alone."

Hannah's heart fell to her stomach. "Oh. I see. Well, never mind. I don't want to bother her. I'll just talk to her at school on Monday."

"Okay. Bye."

"Bye," Hannah said.

So that was why Elsie hadn't called. She didn't want to tell Hannah the bad news. Hannah stood up and paced her room, trying to figure out what to do next. Should she write her camp friends letters and tell them everything? Get it over with? But what if the bracelet mysteriously appeared sometime in the next couple of weeks? Maybe Elsie hadn't looked everywhere at home and someone would find it in a strange place. Like in a shoe. Or between the pages of a book. Or behind the jar of peanut butter.

That was the problem. There were a million places to look, and it would be impossible to look everywhere. If only a magical arrow would appear and point the way.

Hannah decided she had to get out of the house, or she was going to go crazy thinking about the bracelet. She put on her heavy coat and changed into her old boots so she could go out and check on Stardust.

Outside, the temperature had warmed up a bit, and the moon that was almost full looked pretty in the clear, dark sky. Lots of stars twinkled and she wished she had Elsie there to point out another constellation. Instead, she picked the brightest star, stared at it, and made a wish.

Star light, star bright
first star I see tonight
wish I may, wish I might
have the wish I wish tonight.

She closed her eyes and wished for the charm bracelet to come back to her. *Please,* she thought, *please, don't let it be gone forever.*

As she walked to the barn, thinking about the bracelet, she realized the reason she missed it wasn't because it seemed to be lucky sometimes, it was because it made her feel close to her camp friends, Caitlin, Libby, and Mia. The four of them had shared that bracelet, had bought charms for it, and had each taken turns wearing it since they'd left summer camp. It kept them connected in a way nothing else could.

If the bracelet was truly gone, if she couldn't find it, Hannah knew her friends would forever look at her differently. She'd decided they would eventually forgive her, because they were awesome like that, but there would always be that one little thing about Hannah that they couldn't forget. And she just knew things would never be quite the same between the four girls again.

When Hannah reached Stardust's stall, it was as if he'd been waiting for her. He nodded his head at her as she came close, and then lowered it and stepped forward to greet her. Without saying a word, Hannah wrapped her arms around his neck, pressed her check against his soft, warm coat, and let the tears fall.

Chapter 22

CONSTELLATION: Triangulum the Triangle

*M*onday morning at school, Crystal was giving Hannah the cold shoulder. With everything else going on, it was the last thing Hannah wanted to deal with.

"Will you please tell me what I've done wrong?" Hannah asked at their locker before first period. "You're mad at me about something, I can tell."

"I'm not mad," Crystal said matter-of-factly. She looked really cute in a striped white-and-yellow sweater and jeans paired with her blue boots. "I'm just giving you space. You seem like you've got a lot on your mind lately."

"You're right as rain about that," Hannah said with a sigh.

"I remember the good old days, when I used to be your best friend, and you'd *tell* me what was bothering you. But I guess since Elsie's come along . . ."

"Since Elsie's come along, what?" Hannah said, crossing her arms. "What have I done? Tried to be nice to her since her family's struggling while her daddy tries to find a job? Invited her over to ride Stardust because she's the only one who seems to like him? Well, yes, yes I have, and there's no law against any of that, is there? You're still my best friend, Crystal, but geez, I just wish you'd give the girl a chance. I think the three of us could have a lot of fun together."

"She really likes your mule?" Crystal asked.

"Yes," Hannah said. "And just so you know, I do too. I've been riding him lately. Well, not the past few days, because we're letting his hoof heal. But before that, I was riding him. And I can't wait to ride him again."

"You're serious?" Crystal said, looking at Hannah like she'd just told her the sun was green and the sky was orange.

Seeing her best friend, standing there, it was really important to Hannah that Crystal become more involved with what was happening in her life. It seemed that lately, Crystal was like an outsider, looking in. Just thinking about her like that made Hannah upset.

"Yes. And I want you to meet him, and see for yourself that he's really sweet," Hannah said.

"Wait. Does this mean you're inviting me over?" A smile slowly spread across Crystal's face. "Seems like I haven't been to your house in ages."

"I know," said Hannah, realizing she felt the same way. "So I was thinking maybe you'd want to do the science fair with Elsie and me. We're doing an astronomy project. The form is due tomorrow, so I can get it filled out and then the three of us can all meet at my house to talk about the project and make a plan."

Of course, Elsie hadn't gotten back to Hannah yet about whether she wanted to do the project or not. Hannah figured she'd probably just forgotten about it because she'd been so focused on trying to find the bracelet. Well, Hannah figured there was no harm in assuming she wanted to do it if she was able to stay in Soddy-Daisy.

Crystal's smile disappeared when she heard Hannah's suggestion. "That's not what I really had in mind."

"Please don't be like that," Hannah said. "We're going to have a good time!"

Crystal took a deep breath. "Okay. If you say so. But do you promise that one of these days we can do something together, just the two of us? The cake decorating class was so much fun, and I know you would have loved it."

Hannah realized she hadn't even asked Crystal about the class. She'd totally forgotten about it. Suddenly, Hannah felt like a bad friend. Maybe she *had* been kind of ignoring Crystal these past few weeks. She hadn't meant to, of course. It'd just happened, with everything else going on.

"Is there another class at the craft store we could take together?" Hannah asked. "Or maybe we should bake a cake and decorate it, so you can teach me what you learned?"

"I'll have my mom check the schedule and get back to you," Crystal said, her posture relaxing. "I'd love to take a class with you."

Hannah smiled. "That sounds good. In the meantime, the three of us can look at constellations together. It's fun. You'll see."

It wasn't until later that Hannah discovered Elsie wasn't at school. Hannah hoped she wasn't so sick about not finding the bracelet that she'd stayed home to avoid talking about it. She decided it was time to call her and get the awkward conversation over with once and for all.

"Hello?" said a male voice on the other end.

"Hello, is Elsie there?"

"Yes, just a minute, please."

It was only a few seconds before Elsie said, "Hello?"

"Hi, it's me, Hannah."

"Hi."

"Are you . . . okay?" Hannah asked hesitantly. "You weren't at school today."

There was a pause. "Look, I'm sorry I didn't call you. I just couldn't figure out how to tell you that I couldn't find it."

"I know. I figured. And I understand. Is that why you stayed home?"

"No. My dad didn't get the job, so we've started packing. We're moving to Houston in ten days."

Hannah's heart sank. "Oh, Elsie. I'm so sorry."

She didn't say anything for a moment. When Elsie spoke again, her voice was shaky, like she was trying not to cry. "Honestly, it seems like all that bracelet did was bring me bad luck. I wish you'd never given it to me. Why'd you have to go and do that, anyway?"

Hannah couldn't believe what she was hearing. "What? I didn't —"

Elsie interrupted her. "I'm sorry, Hannah, I gotta go. My

mom needs to use the phone. Please tell Stardust I said good-bye. I'm going to miss him." She paused. "And you too. A lot. Bye."

Before Hannah could say anything in return, Elsie hung up.

Chapter 23

CONSTELLATION: Ursa Major
the Great Bear

When Mrs. Crawford called the family down for supper, Hannah decided she wouldn't go. They were having chili and cornbread, and Hannah loved cornbread the way a bear loves fish, but she just didn't feel hungry. She couldn't get Elsie's hurtful words out of her head.

It seems like all that bracelet did was bring me bad luck. I wish you'd never given it to me.

Just as she was about to call downstairs that she didn't feel well, Mr. Crawford walked into Hannah's room.

"I got a surprise for you, sweetie," he said, and handed Hannah a small picture frame with two photos side-by-side. They were the pictures Elsie had taken of Hannah riding Stardust.

As Hannah stared at them, tears filled her eyes. "Wow.

The photos are amazing." She looked at her dad. "Thank you. I love it."

He reached out and wrapped his arms around her. "You're welcome." When he pulled away he gave her a curious look. "You all right?"

Hannah shrugged. "I don't know. It's been a strange afternoon."

"Well, let's go have some supper. Some of that cornbread you love so much will surely cheer you up."

Hannah set the frame on her dresser and decided to do as her father said. Maybe a little bit of food would make her feel better. It certainly didn't seem like it could make her feel any worse.

Everyone else was already seated when Hannah and her father walked into the dining room. Bowls at each place at the table had been filled with chili, and little swirls of steam with a spicy aroma made their way into the air.

"Oh, shoot," Mrs. Crawford said. "I forgot the butter. Hannah, can you grab it, please?"

She went to the fridge and took out the butter dish. When she sat down, she could feel her mother's eyes on her.

"We heard about Elsie," Mrs. Crawford said as she passed the bowl of shredded cheddar cheese to Adam. "It's awful sad news, I know, but I want to tell you something. Today Louanne proposed our little town come together and do something for their family. So we are. This Saturday, at the salon."

Hannah put a napkin in her lap. "What do you mean, do something for them?"

"We're going to hold a fund-raiser. Try and get them enough money to pay the rent they owe. If we can just buy them a little more time, maybe Mr. Weston can find work around here."

"What kind of fund-raiser?" Adam asked while he sprinkled cheese over his chili. Hannah was glad he'd asked, because she was thinking the same thing.

"It was Louanne's idea, and it's a real good one, I think," Mrs. Crawford said. "We're going to turn the salon into a carnival, like the elementary school used to do every year before they decided it wasn't worth the trouble. Silly administrators. Anyway, we'll have a cakewalk, a fishing pond in one of the sinks, a bean bag toss in the other, face painting, and whatever else we can think of."

Eric passed the basket of cornbread to Hannah. "So people will buy tickets?"

"That's right," Mrs. Crawford said. "The more games

and whatnot we can come up with to play, the more tickets we can sell. So put your thinking caps on."

"You should use the parking lot too," Eric said. "Lots of space out there, if you ask people to park on the street and walk over."

"That's a great idea," Mr. Crawford said. "I know a guy who rents out bouncy houses. Could probably get him to donate a rental for the day."

Hannah's eyes got big. "What if we offered a mule ride? And maybe for extra money, people could pay to get their pictures taken?"

Mr. Crawford raised one of his eyebrows. It was a special skill he liked to show off whenever possible. "Now that's an interesting idea."

Eric slurped a spoonful of chili and then said, "You sure people will want to pay to ride him? You might have to pay *them* to give him a chance."

Hannah gave him a dirty look. "Stop it. That's not nice."

"I think this might be an excellent way for people to see a mule is just as good, if not better, than riding a horse," Mr. Crawford said, taking a piece of cornbread from the basket and putting it on his plate. "As both Hannah and I know, he rides like a dream, and photographs like one too."

"You sure his hoof will be healed in time?" Mrs. Crawford asked.

"When I'm done eating, I'll go over and talk to Grandpa about it," Hannah replied. "Far as I know, he should be good to go."

"Well, regardless of what we decide about Stardust, I'll need everyone's help getting the place ready Friday night," Mrs. Crawford said. "And between now and then, Hannah, maybe you can help me call folks and get donations for the cakewalk and prizes for the games and whatnot."

"Sure," Hannah said. "I'll do anything I can to help."

"Let me take care of the advertising," Mr. Crawford said. "I'll call the newspapers tomorrow and a few radio stations as well."

Mrs. Crawford gave her husband an appreciative look as she took a bite of her chili.

"When are you going to tell the Westons you're doing this?" Hannah asked. "Because they're already starting to pack, and are planning to leave next week."

Her mother nodded. "You want to go over there with me after supper? Give them the news?"

Hannah told herself Elsie might not be happy to see her at first, but she'd come around when she found out why they were paying them a visit. "Sure. I'll go with you. But Mama, what if it's not enough? What if we go to all this trouble, but we don't raise enough money, and they still have to move?"

Her mother raised both arms up and crossed her fingers. "All we can do is hope that Lady Luck is on our side and everything works out."

That was not what Hannah wanted to hear, since Lady Luck did *not* seem to be on her side lately. At all.

Chapter 24

Constellation: Pisces
the Fishes

The week was a whirlwind of activity, getting ready for the carnival. Every day after school, Hannah was busy doing something to help the ladies of Beauty by Design so they'd have less on their to-do lists. Thursday morning, Mrs. Crawford told Hannah she was "pleased as punch" about how well things were coming along in such a short amount of time. Hannah was happy, too, especially because Elsie was back at school, since the Westons were feeling hopeful, and extremely grateful, about the fund-raiser.

When Hannah and her mother had gone to Elsie's house to tell them about the fund-raiser, the entire Weston family could hardly believe the news. After it finally sunk in, Mrs. Weston had asked, "How will we ever be able to repay you?"

Mrs. Crawford had simply said that was what folks do — they helped each other when they needed it. As Hannah had turned to leave when it was time to go, Elsie stepped forward and gave her a big hug. She didn't say anything, but she didn't really need to. Hannah understood that it'd been a stressful couple of weeks, and what Elsie had said earlier was probably a result of all that stress.

At school, Hannah and Crystal were eating lunch together again, as usual. They sat at their normal table and shared a bag of potato chips as they ate the sandwiches they'd each brought.

"Are you going to come to the carnival on Saturday?" Hannah asked.

"Probably," Crystal said. "Braden really wants to go. He's been bugging my parents for a puppy, and they want to get him a goldfish instead. They told him it's a much better pet for an eight-year-old. Easier to take care of and all that. Will you be giving away plastic bags of fish like they used to do at the elementary school carnival?"

"No," Hannah said. "We checked into it, but we decided not to. Braden can ride Stardust though. We're bringing him along and letting people ride him around the parking lot for the price of two tickets. His hoof healed up just fine."

Crystal picked up a chip and munched on it. "That's good, but riding a mule is not quite the same thing as getting a puppy," she teased.

"And a goldfish is?" Hannah said with a smile.

"Well, it's a pet, at least. But you're right, it's not really the same. You can't cuddle with a goldfish. Can't walk a goldfish. Can't play fetch with a goldfish. I'm not sure what my parents are thinking, exactly."

"They're thinking a goldfish is a million times easier than a puppy, and that's all that matters."

Crystal nodded. "Yep. Sounds about right."

"Hey," Hannah said, setting her sandwich down on the plastic baggie. "Do you want to come over Sunday so we can start planning the science fair project?"

"Sure," Crystal said. "Think you'll still have some energy left after that busy day on Saturday?"

A day doing nothing did sound pretty nice, Hannah thought. But she was anxious to bring Crystal and Elsie together so they could get to know each other better. Especially now that it looked like Elsie might stay on in Soddy-Daisy a little while longer.

"Yeah, I'll be fine. It's not like we're going out to plow the fields. We'll be talking about stars. Beautiful, magical stars. That won't be too tiring, right?"

"If you say so," Crystal said, before she took another bite of her peanut butter and honey sandwich. She finished chewing and then asked, "Hannah, are you worried about what happens if no one comes to the carnival?"

"We just can't think like that." Hannah put her elbows on the table and squeezed her hands together. "People have to come. And they have to buy lots of tickets and fill up the donation jars we're setting out too."

Crystal leaned in, almost whispering. "But what if they don't?"

Hannah had asked herself that question at least a dozen times. It would be terrible if they had to tell Elsie's family that the carnival was a failure when it was all over, which would probably mean they'd have to move after all. She just kept telling herself that everything would work out.

"Did I tell you I lost the charm bracelet I got at camp?" Hannah decided it was time to change the subject.

Crystal's mouth dropped open. "No. What happened? I mean, where'd you lose it?"

"I don't know. I let Elsie borrow it and we think she lost it at church and someone picked it up there."

"Have you told your camp friends?"

"No. I keep hoping someone will turn it in to the office at the church. I haven't written to any of my camp friends in a while. First it was because I didn't want to tell them about Stardust. But now that I don't care about that, I can't write to them until we find the bracelet. If we ever find the bracelet, that is. I feel so bad."

"And I feel bad for you," Crystal said. She reached into her lunch bag and pulled out two homemade chocolate chip cookies. "Here, you want one of these? Chocolate always makes me feel better."

"You know I can't turn down a cookie." She reached her hand out as Crystal opened the baggie and let Hannah take one. "Did you make them?"

"Are you kidding me? You're the baker I wish I could be. No, my mama and Braden made them together after school yesterday. They're good, I promise. And by the way, I found a class for us to take at the craft store."

"You did? What is it?"

"We're going to learn how to make bath and beauty products. You know, like bath salts, body lotions, hand creams. That kind of stuff."

Hannah's eyes got big. "We are?"

Crystal laughed. "Yes, ma'am. We sure are. It's not this weekend, but the next. Just in time for Valentine's Day. All the boys will be swarming us when they get a whiff of our lovely creations."

"You're crazy, Crystal. It'd have to be body lotion with super magical powers to make that happen."

"Anyway," she continued, "there's a fee of twelve dollars that covers the cost of supplies, and then you'll bring home a basket full of stuff plus the recipes so you can make them again if you want to."

"That sounds good," Hannah said. "And in the meantime, we have the carnival and stargazing to look forward to."

"You better wish on a star that your special bracelet shows up," Crystal said, popping a bite of the cookie into her mouth.

"I already have. Believe me."

Crystal shrugged. "Well, don't give up yet. Sometimes magic takes time."

Chapter 25

CONSTELLATION: Cepheus
the King

Friday night, Hannah and her family were busier than a king and queen on coronation day. Transforming a beauty parlor into a carnival was no small feat. But with the help of a few card tables, cardboard, and lots of construction paper, they managed to do a decent job. The receptionist desk was where Hannah would sit the following day, selling tickets. She'd covered it in red construction paper and made a sign explaining the pricing options. Another sign read:

Help the Weston family stay in Soddy-Daisy.
Every dime made at the carnival will go to them.
Thank you for your support!

She'd decorated ten canning jars and placed them around the shop for donations as well. Along with games set up on the card tables, and a cakewalk in the very back of the shop, each of the styling stations had a game to play too. The one at her grandma's station was Hannah's favorite: the Soda Pop Toss. They'd set up a bunch of Coke bottles in a triangle shape and the goal was to sit in the chair and toss a hard plastic ring so it would fall down onto one of glass bottles perfectly and rest around the neck of the bottle. Hannah had tried it at least a dozen times, and only once had she managed to "ring" a bottle.

As for Stardust, her father and grandfather had volunteered to come along on Saturday and be in charge of the rides and photos. Her grandma had kept an old Polaroid instant camera, so they could take a picture and wait a minute and be able to hand it to the customer right then and there. Stardust would walk the perimeter of the parking lot, while a big bouncy house would sit in the middle of it.

Hannah knew they'd done everything they could think of to make the carnival fun. Now, it was up to the town of Soddy-Daisy as to whether or not it was a success.

As they finished up their work Friday night, Hannah went into the back of the shop, where Louanne was busy unwrapping prizes and putting them in various buckets to have at each of the game stations.

"Hi, Louanne," she said.

"Hey there," Louanne replied, tossing her blond hair back as she looked up. "It's looking real good out there. Think it's gonna be a blast, don't you?"

"Yep. As long as people show up."

"They will," Louanne said, examining a big, sparkly bouncy ball. "We live in a fine community." She smiled at Hannah. "We look out for each other, you know?"

"I know," Hannah said. "Thanks for coming up with the idea to do this for them."

Louanne waved her hand in the air. "No thanks necessary, hon. Rosie's been a client of mine for a long time. I'm worried about them same as you are, and would hate to see them have to move."

Hannah nodded.

Louanne dropped the bouncy ball into a bucket and then walked closer to Hannah. "I don't judge them for the problems they're going through, you know. I feel bad for them, that's all."

"I know," Hannah said, even if she wasn't sure whether this was exactly true or not.

"I'm not always the kind of person I'd like to be," Louanne continued. "Not like your mother, who is probably the sweetest woman this side of the Mississippi. But I'm trying. Ever since you and your mama came over that night and showed me a whole lot of kindness when I really needed it, I'm trying hard." She looked down at her hands and picked at one of her fingernails. "Even if sometimes it might not seem like it, I am trying."

Hannah wasn't sure what to say.

"Anyway," Louanne said, reaching down and picking up a neon orange bucket. "I just wanted you to know that." She handed the bucket to Hannah. "Want to help me put the rest of these prizes in these buckets? Then I think we're about done for the night."

"Sure," Hannah said. "I'd love to."

The next morning, Hannah got up, threw on some clothes, and went outside to help her father and grandfather get Stardust loaded into the old horse trailer her grandparents owned. It had rained the night before, so the air smelled fresh and clean, and the ground was damp. She stepped around a couple of small puddles, hoping it wouldn't rain today. A mule ride wouldn't be nearly as fun in the rain.

As Hannah had suspected, Stardust didn't give them a bit of trouble, just stepped right into the trailer like it was his stall in the barn. Because of the preparations for the carnival, Hannah had only ridden him once since her grandpa had given the okay. His hoof seemed to be fine, though, and he was walking normally again.

"I reckon I should change into something a bit more presentable," her grandpa said with a slight grin. He had on old jeans, his favorite wool coat, and the straw hat.

"Yup, me too," Mr. Crawford said. "Meet you out here in fifteen minutes or so?"

"Sounds good," Grandpa said. "That gives me enough time to have a bite to eat too." He looked at Hannah. "Your grandmother stayed up into the wee hours of the morning baking up goodies for the cakewalk. Along with three different kinds of cake, we've got pumpkin bread and banana bread too. When people see those goodies, they'll buy lots of tickets for sure. We'll see if she makes me pay for a piece of bread and butter for my breakfast."

"Guess I better bring some money along then, just in case," Hannah said with a smile. "I want some of that banana bread myself!"

"See you soon," he called out as he turned away.

Hannah turned and followed her daddy toward their house. "What about you, Hannah?" he asked. "You gonna ride into town with us or wait and go with your mama?"

"I'll go with Mama, Grandma, and the twins," Hannah said. "I want to take a shower and have Mama put my hair in a braid. It'll be nice to have it out of the way today."

"I have a good feeling about today," he said as put his arm around his daughter's shoulders. "A real good feeling."

It was just what Hannah needed to hear, to put her mind at ease. For a little while, anyway.

An hour later, as Hannah and her mother were slipping on their coats, waiting for Adam and Eric to come downstairs, Mrs. Crawford's cell phone rang. She pulled it out of her purse and checked the number.

"It's your daddy," she said as she pressed TALK. "Hi, Anthony. Everything all right?"

Hannah watched her mother's face as Mrs. Crawford listened to her husband talk. When the corners of her mouth turned down, Hannah knew there was trouble.

"Oh, Anthony, I'm so sorry that happened. Are you sure he's all right?" Mrs. Crawford turned to Hannah and gave her a concerned look. "Yes, I'll talk to your mother and see what we want to do. I'm guessing we'll ride separately now, so she can go to the hospital. Unless you think we should all be there."

At the mention of the word *hospital* Hannah's knees began to shake. Then Adam and Eric appeared.

"What's wrong?" Eric asked. "You look like you're going to be sick."

"Someone's at the hospital," Hannah said.

"What?" Adam asked, turning to their mother. "Mom, what's going on?"

Mrs. Crawford held up her finger. "All right. We'll see you later. Yes, I'll tell her. Good-bye."

"What is it?" Hannah asked, trying to keep the panic she felt under control. "What's wrong?"

Mrs. Crawford put her hand on Hannah's shoulder. "Well, it's bad news, I'm afraid. A few men were putting up the bouncy house when your grandpa and daddy arrived. You know, blowing it up with air or whatever it is they do. As the two of them were leading Stardust out of the trailer, he got spooked real bad."

"What do you mean? What happened?"

Her mother swallowed hard. "Stardust kicked your grandpa. Your daddy said it could have been much worse, that his hoof just grazed him, but they kick mighty hard, and he's afraid he might have broken a rib or two. Your daddy called for an ambulance, and while they waited for it to arrive, he got Stardust back in the trailer. They're taking Grandpa to X-ray now."

"Oh no," Hannah said. "Poor Grandpa. And poor Stardust. I hate the idea of him being so scared he'd do something like that."

"Poor Stardust?" Adam said. "He's not the one we should be worried about right now. Grandpa is in the hospital, Hannah."

She turned and glared at her brother. "I know that. But can't I feel bad for Stardust too?"

"It worries me, Hannah," her mama said, rubbing her hands together nervously. "That he went and did something like that. I'm not sure I feel comfortable having you around him after this."

Hannah's mouth dropped open. "Mama, it was a one-time thing."

"Well, your daddy and I need to talk about it. I'm not sure what we're going to do, to be honest."

"What we're going to do," Hannah said, trying not to cry, "is go to the carnival, and I'm going to walk Stardust around that parking lot so many times that bouncy house doesn't faze him one bit."

Mrs. Crawford shook her head hard. "No. No you are not. No one is getting on that mule today; it's out of the question."

"But that's so —"

"No buts," Mrs. Crawford said, heading toward the door. "Come on. We need to go talk to Grandma. Your father has surely called her by now and she's probably worried sick."

"Are we going to the hospital?" Eric asked.

"No," Mrs. Crawford replied. "The show, or carnival in this case, must go on. Your father wants us to see it through. There's nothing we can do for Grandpa right now, anyway, and he's certainly in good hands."

As they stepped outside, Hannah knew her mom was right. Grandpa was in good hands. She wished she could say the same for Stardust. It made her sad, thinking of him all alone in that trailer, scared and confused. She had to see him. She just had to.

Chapter 26

Constellation: Chamaeleon the Chameleon

They arrived at the beauty shop at ten o'clock, an hour before the carnival was scheduled to open. Adam and Eric had asked a few of their friends to come and assist with the games, and Louanne had asked her two teenage nieces to come and help out as well. Mrs. Crawford went to work explaining each of the stations and how the tickets and prizes would work. She'd asked Hannah to set up the baked goods table next to the ticket counter with a sign that explained the cakewalk was in the back, and every winner got to pick something from the table. A bunch of people had dropped off goodies the night before, so along with her grandma's stuff, there were a lot of items to spread out.

Still, it didn't take Hannah too long to do the work. When she was finished setting up, she glanced behind her and saw that her mother and all of the kids were occupied at one of the stations. Louanne was in the back room. Hannah knew this was her only chance.

She snuck out the front door and walked around to the large parking lot in back. The bouncy house, which looked like a large castle, was completely inflated. The men who had been there to set it up were gone. On the far side of the lot was the truck and horse trailer. As soon as she spotted it, Hannah ran toward the trailer. There were small windows up by the mule's head, and she could see him looking at her.

"It's okay, Stardust," she said. "Everything's all right. I know you didn't mean it. It wasn't your fault. You just got scared, that's all."

"Spooked him good, that's for sure." Hannah spun around, surprised to see her daddy standing there. She rushed over and gave him a hug.

"What are you doing here?" she asked him when she pulled away. "What about Grandpa?"

"Nothing's broken, thank goodness," he explained. "Just bruised. He's gonna be sore for a few days, that's for sure. But he's got a prescription to help with the pain and Grandma's taken him home to rest. Figured y'all could use my help over here."

"Can we get him out of the trailer?" Hannah asked. "He's been in there a long time, and I'm worried he's upset with us. I want to show him there's nothing to be afraid of, and that I'm not mad at him."

He sighed. "I don't know, honey. Your grandpa is a lucky man. It could very well happen again."

"What happened is as much our fault as it is his. We should have realized the bouncy house would be new to him. We should have prepared him somehow."

"You're right," Mr. Crawford said. "We probably should have gotten some colorful nylon material and hung it around the farm and made him walk around it. But we didn't. And I'm just afraid it's too late to do anything about it now."

Hannah bit her lip as tears pricked her eyes. "Mama thinks the worst of him. She doesn't want me anywhere near him. We have to change her mind. To show her that everything's okay and he's not as bad as she thinks he is right now. Please, daddy. Please?"

Mr. Crawford scratched his scruffy chin and stared at the horse trailer. Then he turned and looked back at the shop. "All right. Let's get him out here and see what happens."

Hannah reached up and gave him another hug. "Thanks, Daddy. Thank you so much."

He shook his head. "Are you sure you're the same girl who was complaining about this here mule not too long ago?"

"I'm the same girl, I just see things differently now, that's all."

"Okay, let me see if I can get him out of that trailer. You stand back, you hear me?"

"If you say so," Hannah said. "I'm going to talk to him, though. I want to let him know I'm right here and there's nothing to be afraid of."

And that's exactly what she did. While Mr. Crawford slowly led Stardust out of the trailer, Hannah stood to the side and gently encouraged him with her voice. Once the mule was completely out, and standing on the pavement of the parking lot, Hannah slowly approached him.

"That was awesome," she told him. "You just backed out of there like you'd done it a million times. Because there's nothing to be afraid of, isn't that right?" She patted Stardust's neck as she turned and spoke to her father. "Can we walk him around the bouncy house and see how he acts?"

"Even if he does well, Hannah, I'm thinking it's probably not wise to put strange kids on him today. There's too much of a risk."

"Can I ride him, real quick like?" she asked.

"You know your mother would have my hide if I did that. But I'll do my best to convince her to let you ride him later today, if there's time."

"You gonna take him back home, then?" Hannah asked. "I don't like the idea of him staying in that trailer for the next few hours."

"Yep. I'll take him home and then I'll come back and help out here however I can."

Just then, Mrs. Crawford walked up. "What in the world are the two of you doing? Haven't we had enough trouble for one day?"

"I wanted to show you that everything's fine, Mama. See?" She patted Stardust's neck, and he turned his head and looked at Mrs. Crawford. "He did great coming out of the trailer. Daddy says we can't risk having anyone ride him after what happened, though, and I understand. But I'm planning on riding him when we get home later today. And again tomorrow when Elsie and Crystal come over."

Mrs. Crawford looked at her husband. "I don't like this idea very much."

"I think it'll be fine," he replied. "If it makes you feel better, I'll ride him first to make sure everything's all right."

"Your mother called me," Mrs. Crawford said to Mr. Crawford. "Told me they were heading home to rest. I'm glad nothing's broken." She looked at Hannah. "It could have been so much worse. We can't take this lightly. We need to sit down and have a long conversation about this when we have more time. But right now, people are arriving. There's a line by the front door. So, what I need you to do right now is go inside and get ready to sell tickets. Can you do that for me, please?"

There was so much Hannah wanted to say, but she knew this wasn't the time. "Yes, ma'am. I can do that."

Hannah turned to give Stardust one last pat, when a group of people walked up to them. Not just any group of people — Mr. Brody and some of the kids from the 4-H club.

"Hey, Hannah," Mr. Brody said. "We came out to support your fund-raiser. It's a great thing, what y'all are doing for the Westons."

"Oh, well, thanks so much for coming," she replied.

"What's the mule doing here?" Carson asked.

Hannah spoke up quickly, before either of her parents had a chance to respond. She didn't want them to mention what had happened to her grandpa. It might make them think even less of Stardust. "We were going to let people ride him and get their pictures taken, but he got kind of spooked by the bouncy house."

Mr. Brody walked over and let Stardust sniff his hand before he gently stroked his neck. "That's too bad, though I've seen it happen many times over the years. And I certainly understand your hesitation. Better to be safe than sorry."

"Aw, I wanted to ride him," Darren said. "I'm curious if it's the same as riding a horse."

"Yeah, me too," Mary Beth said.

Hannah couldn't believe what she was hearing. They didn't like Stardust. Did they?

"I have an idea," Mr. Brody said. "How about at our next riding meeting, we let people take turns riding Stardust? And then at the following educational meeting, we compare mules and horses, discussing the ways they are both different and similar." He looked at Mr. Crawford. "If that's all right with you, of course."

"I think that's a fine idea," Mr. Crawford said. "Hannah sure likes riding him, and I bet the rest of the kids will feel the same."

"Actually," Mrs. Crawford said with authority in her voice, "we're not sure at this point in time if Hannah will be keeping Stardust."

"Sarah," Mr. Crawford said, "That's a little extreme, don't you think? We're going to discuss the situation, remember?"

There was a moment of awkward silence before Mr. Brody said, "Well, I hope everything works out. One of the things I planned on doing while I was here was to let you know that we'd love to have Hannah and Stardust ride in the Valentine's Day parade with us."

This news should have made Hannah jump for joy. It was a childhood dream, finally coming true. Except, because of a silly bouncy house, her dream might not come true at all.

Chapter 27

CONSTELLATION: Telescopium
the Telescope

That night, Hannah lay in her bed, turning over the events of the day in her mind. The carnival had been a huge success. They'd raised lots of money for the Westons, but not only that, three different people from Chattanooga had left their business cards asking Mr. Weston to call them to inquire about positions they had available at their companies. When the Westons had stopped in to see the carnival for themselves and to thank everyone for their hard work, Mrs. Crawford gave them the good news about the results of the fund-raiser and the job prospects Mr. Weston now had. Elsie's parents had stood there in awe, struggling not to cry.

"Thank you so much," Elsie had told Hannah when she pulled her away for a second to talk to her in private. "For everything. I'm really sorry about getting mad at you last week. I shouldn't have done that. You've done nothing but help me. You're a good friend, Hannah."

"I'm so glad everything's looking up for y'all," Hannah had said.

Of course, what she hadn't said was how badly things were going for Hannah. The bracelet hadn't turned up, and now there was a possibility she could lose Stardust too.

After the carnival was over, at two, the Crawford family had spent a couple of hours getting the beauty shop back to normal. When they were finished, everyone was starving. Adam and Eric convinced Mr. Crawford to take the family out to eat at Fries and Pies. Normally, Hannah would have been thrilled about this, but she was too upset worrying about Stardust to eat much.

When they'd gotten home, Mrs. Crawford said that after the long, hard day they'd had, they were going to visit Grandpa and Grandma for a little while, and then settle in for a family movie night. Hannah had tried to protest, wanting to go out and at least see Stardust, but her mother had been firm. "Hannah, I'm tired. I don't want to discuss this right now. Your father can feed him tonight."

Her daddy had tried to reassure her. "We'll talk tomorrow, all right? Try not to worry. Everything's going to work out."

Now, Hannah tossed and turned, wondering what they would decide to do. She understood that her mother was worried, that she thought she was looking out for Hannah, trying to prevent her from getting hurt. But she didn't know Stardust the way Hannah did. Hannah knew for certain he hadn't meant to hurt her grandpa. It'd been an accident. It could have happened with any horse or mule, and that's what she had to get her mother to understand.

Across the room, a little bit of light slipped through the crack where the curtains met up in the middle of the window. Hannah got up and pulled the curtains back. The light came from the half-moon in the sky. Stars twinkled around it, and she thought back to the night she'd decided to name the mule Stardust. Now, more than ever, she needed a little of that magic Elsie had talked about.

The stars seemed to be calling her name, as if they wanted to help her. She knew she should get back in bed and go to sleep. But that's not what she did. Instead, she got dressed, grabbed a flashlight from a drawer in the kitchen, and walked out into the cool night air.

She studied the night sky as she headed toward the barn, walking slowly so she wouldn't trip on anything. When she saw the light streak across the sky, she let out a gasp and stopped, frozen in place.

A falling star. She'd seen a falling star! Quickly, she closed her eyes and made a wish.

I know I didn't like Stardust at first, but I like him now. I think I even love him, and I don't want him to go. I don't want to lose him like I lost the bracelet. Please, let him stay.

After wishing on the star, she made her way to the barn. Once inside, she shut the doors and turned on all of the lights. She couldn't get to Stardust fast enough. When he saw her, he nodded his head and swished his tail, as if to say hello. She cozied up to his head and stroked his face. "I know you didn't mean to do it," she whispered. "I'm not mad. I promise."

She wanted to ride him so badly. To let him know that as far as she was concerned, nothing had changed. But it was dark outside and she knew she'd get into huge trouble if she got caught.

"How about if I brush you?" she said to him.

She opened the door to his stall and led him out to the

place he always stood to be brushed and saddled. "Stay here while I get the brush," she told him.

As she walked to the shelf where the brush was stored, she heard something. She turned around to find that Stardust had backed up a few feet, so his rear end was practically resting up against the barn doors.

"Hey," Hannah called out. "What are you doing?" She quickly grabbed the brush before she returned to his left side. "You want to go outside? Is that it? I'm sorry, but we can't. Not tonight. Now come on, let's get you back where you belong."

But he stood there, and when she tried to get him to move forward, he wouldn't move. "What's wrong, boy?" she asked. "What is it?"

He picked up his front right hoof and then set it back down, though not all the way. It was the one that had been hurt, and Hannah wondered if it was bothering him again. She moved around so she stood in front of him and looked down at his right hoof. And that's when she saw something shiny, barely sticking out from beneath the wooden door that made up one of the stalls on the right side of the barn.

"It can't be, can it?" she whispered as she reached down and pulled on it.

It came out in one piece and everything was there, looking just as adorable as ever.

The charm bracelet.

Hannah threw the brush down and wrapped her arms around Stardust's neck. "You found it for me. Thank you, thank you, thank you." She laughed as she thought of the bracelet here, in the barn, this whole time. It must have fallen off of Elsie's wrist when they'd come to the barn that Saturday to ride Stardust. For a second, she wondered if Stardust had originally stepped on the bracelet and that's what caused the small hole in his hoof. But given the position of the bracelet, that seemed unlikely. It was still in perfect condition too.

She stuffed the bracelet into her pocket and went back to the task at hand. After he was brushed and back in his stall, Hannah told him, "Everything's going to be okay. I'm sure of it. I saw a falling star and you found the lucky bracelet. Luck is on our side now. I can feel it."

Hannah was so happy, it seemed as if she floated back to the house on a magical star. Back inside her room, she took the bracelet out of her pocket and clasped it onto her wrist.

A memory came to mind of Caitlin, Mia, Libby, and Hannah standing at the counter of the Pink Giraffe, gathering their money to pay for the bracelet. They'd been so excited to find something that sealed their friendship. Something they could pass around and share during the time they couldn't physically be together. Hannah had been worried she'd ruined it all, but the bracelet was back. Tomorrow night, after she spent time with Elsie and Crystal, Hannah would make sure to write each of her camp friends a letter. They were probably starting to worry because she hadn't written them in so long.

But for now, she crawled into bed and fell asleep with a smile on her face.

The next morning, the family went to church and then returned home to have lunch and do chores.

As they sat at the dining table finishing up their soup and sandwiches, Hannah decided she couldn't wait any longer. "Um, Elsie and Crystal are coming over so we can work on our science fair project."

"Oh, that sounds like fun," her daddy said. "What's the project?"

"We're going to see if changes in the moon affect how well you can see the stars. Today we'll plan everything out.

The stargazing will come later. Anyway, I was wondering, while they're here, if we could also —"

Mrs. Crawford interrupted her. "You're going to ask about riding Stardust, aren't you?"

Hannah gulped and fingered the charm bracelet. This was it. If the bracelet was lucky, she needed it to work now more than ever. "Yes."

Mrs. Crawford set her spoon down and pushed her soup bowl to the side. She folded her hands and placed them in front of her, on the table. "Sweetheart, your grandpa made sure to tell me last night that I shouldn't be too hard on Stardust. That it wasn't his fault. He said he and your daddy should have realized how awful and scary that bouncy house must have looked to the mule."

"Do you think he's right?" Hannah asked, holding her breath.

Mrs. Crawford looked at Mr. Crawford. She didn't say anything for a moment. "Do you trust him?" she asked her husband. "The mule, I mean."

"One hundred percent," he replied without any hesitation.

She turned back to Hannah. "Yes. I think your grandpa is right. And I think you two are going to look mighty fine in the Valentine's Day parade."

Hannah jumped up and ran over to her mother's chair and threw her arms around her neck as she gave her a kiss on her cheek. "Thanks, Mama. Thank you so much."

"You're welcome!"

"Daddy, can we go get him saddled up? The girls will be here soon."

He stood up. "You bet your boots we can."

When Elsie arrived a little while later, Hannah ran to the driveway to greet her. "You're not going to believe what I found," she said, holding her wrist out for her to see.

Elsie's eyes got big and round. "No way."

"Yes, way," she said.

Just then, Crystal's mom pulled up and Crystal jumped out of the car and ran over to where Elsie and Hannah were standing.

"I was just about to tell Elsie how I found the lost bracelet," she told Crystal.

Crystal's hand flew to her mouth. "I'm so happy you found it. What happened?"

Hannah told them about how she saw the falling star and made a wish, and how then she went into the barn and

Stardust showed her where the bracelet had been hiding the whole time.

"That is amazing," Crystal said. "It was here the whole time."

"I can't believe you saw a falling star last night," Elsie said. "I'm so jealous."

"It was one of the most magical moments of my life," Hannah said. "I wish you both could have been there with me. Next week I'm going to ask Mama to take me into town so I can get a charm for the bracelet. It's my turn to add something to it. Can you guess what kind of charm I'm going to get?"

At the exact same time, both Elsie and Crystal said, "A star!"

The three girls giggled. "Ding, ding, ding," Hannah said. "You win the prize!"

"Which is what?" Crystal asked.

"How about a ride on a fantastic mule?"

"Sounds good to me," Elsie said. "Do you want to ride first or talk about our project first?"

"I'm pretty sure I know what Hannah wants to do," Crystal said. "Seeing as how Stardust is basically her hero right about now."

Before Hannah could respond, her father called from the front door. "Hey, I just remembered, I have an old telescope in the attic. Want me to pull it down for you to use?"

"Okay," Hannah said, smiling. "We'll be inside later to check it out. Right now, we have our own special Stardust right here who deserves our attention."

And with that, they took off running toward the barn.

Six months later

$\mathcal{T}$he four girls took their spots in the friendship circle underneath the pine trees. It was the first time they'd had friendship circle since they'd returned to Camp Brookridge. The sweet smell of pine filled the air around them. Hannah silently wondered if the smell of pine would always remind her of friendship circle. She hoped it would.

"Welcome to another meeting in the friendship circle," Caitlin said. "As it's been since the beginning, our friendship circle is secret, safe, and special. Speak your mind, but please be kind. And always remember . . ."

Hannah, Mia, and Libby joined in, with lots of enthusiasm. "No matter what, wherever we go, we're friends forever, this we know."

The girls held up their arms and cheered. Then they all laughed.

"It's sooooo good to be back here with y'all again," Hannah said, resting her elbows on her knees. "I missed you girls something awful."

"Me too," Mia said with a slight grin. "I was a little worried for a while I wouldn't make it back here. But everything worked out."

"Awesome," Caitlin said, and the girls laughed, because it was the perfect word to say to Mia.

"Is that still your favorite word?" Libby asked Mia. "Or do you have a new one?"

"I still love it," Mia said. "Except I do like that word you used in one of your letters to me. It's a funny little word one of your friends likes to say. Do you remember?"

"Of course," Libby said. "How could I forget? Everything is *nifty* to Sabrina."

"Nifty," Hannah said, trying on the word for size. "I like it. Sounds like something you'd hear at the beauty shop back home."

"You know what I think is nifty?" Caitlin asked with a twinkle in her pretty brown eyes.

"What?" the three girls said in unison.

Caitlin reached over and took Hannah's arm and lifted it in the air. "Our bracelet. Don't you guys love how it turned out, with the four charms we picked out?"

"I'm so glad there was enough time to send it around again, so we each could wear it once more, with all of the charms on it," Mia said. "When I wore it the first time, it only had the flower charm that Caitlin had bought."

"Well, when I wore it home from camp, there weren't any charms," Caitlin said. "What did you say, Hannah, about the bracelet not having any charms?"

"I believe I said, it looked as sad as a dog without a bone."

Caitlin laughed. "Yep. That's what you said, all right."

"I got so many compliments on it when I wore it with all four charms," Libby said. "I don't think I could have gotten any more compliments if I'd been wearing a tiara."

"Oooh, that'd be fun," Hannah said. "Should we get one of those to pass around next year?"

"It wouldn't be very easy to mail," Caitlin pointed out.

"I'm pretty sure surfing while wearing a tiara is illegal," Mia said, as she reached back and tightened her ponytail. "And if it isn't, it should be."

Everyone laughed.

"No, I think we should stick to our lucky bracelet," Mia said.

"The question is," Hannah said softly, "do we *really* think it's lucky?"

"If we had our camp journals, that could be our question of the day," Caitlin said.

"But we haven't been to the arts-and-crafts building yet," Libby said. "So we're just going to have to go around the circle and say if we think it's lucky or not, and why."

"Is everyone okay with that?" Caitlin asked.

The girls nodded.

"Okay, who wants to start?"

Hannah spoke up. "For a long time, I wasn't sure if it was lucky. But I think it is. As you all know, since I wrote to you about it, I lost it for a little while, but when I finally found it again, my friend Elsie got to stay in Soddy-Daisy because her dad found a job. I was able to keep Stardust even after something terrible happened. And, I rode in the Valentine's Day parade, which was *so* much fun, you guys. More fun than a kid in a bouncy house, I'm telling you what."

"Yeah," Mia said. "I think it's lucky too. Lacy Bell and I have the best time going bird watching together. I think the lucky bracelet helped bring us together."

"That's how I feel about my friends at school," Caitlin said. "Like, I didn't win the election while I had the bracelet, but in the end, it wasn't that important to me anyway. What really mattered was making friends. And I ended up with a couple of great ones."

"Me too," Libby said, nodding. "That's how I feel about Cedric and Sabrina." She paused. "But lucky or not, it doesn't really matter that much, right?"

"What do you mean?" Hannah asked.

"We have each other," Libby explained in her adorable British accent. "And we'll always have each other, whether we have the bracelet or not. That's not just lucky."

She paused and looked around at each of her friends.

"It's awesome," Mia said, jumping in.

"Nifty," Libby said, smiling.

"Better than dozens of gorgeous flowers," Caitlin said.

"More amazing than a shooting star," Hannah said.

And so it was, as the best of friendships always are.

Four Best Friends, One
Charmed Life

Charmed Life — Caitlin's Lucky Charm — LISA SCHROEDER

Charmed Life — Mia's Golden Bird — LISA SCHROEDER

Charmed Life — Libby's Sweet Surprise — LISA SCHROEDER

Charmed Life — Hannah's Bright Star — LISA SCHROEDER

Caitlin, Mia, Libby, and Hannah became best friends forever at camp, but now they have to go their separate ways. Luckily, they have a very special charm bracelet to share. As they mail it back and forth, each girl will receive it just when she needs it the most!

SCHOLASTIC
scholastic.com

Available in print and eBook editions.

Four girls, one bracelet, and a little bit of luck . . .

Caitlin's life at summer camp with her new best friends — Hannah, Mia, and Libby — is charmed. But at home? Caitlin's dad might be losing his job, her mom is making her do volunteer work, and Caitlin's going to a new school, where none of the girls are as fun or friendly as her Cabin 7 BFFs. At least Caitlin has a good-luck charm — a good-luck charm *bracelet*. The Cabin 7 girls bought it together, and Caitlin is taking the first turn wearing it. She's sure it will help . . . but when?

Charmed Life

Mia's Golden Bird

LISA SCHROEDER

Scholastic

$\mathcal{M}$ia loves two things: surfing and photography. When she breaks her foot, she tries to stay busy making scrapbooks, but she's still bored. Then one day Mia's photos catch someone's eye: the famous actress Lacy Bell! Lacy is a bird-watcher with her grandmother and offers to pay Mia to be their photographer! It's perfect — until the kids at school start gossiping. Mia's glad she has her lucky charm bracelet — she's going to need it!

Charmed Life

Libby's Sweet Surprise

LISA SCHROEDER

📖SCHOLASTIC

When she's not at her family's sweets shop, Libby loves walking her dog. Especially because she always meets interesting people — like Cedric, another dog owner her age. When Libby finds out Cedric's family owns a new candy store in town, she tries to keep her family business a secret. She really likes Cedric and wants to be his friend. But the truth has to come out . . . and Libby will need her BFFs' lucky charm bracelet's help!

Read all of Hayley's confessions – you're in for a treat!

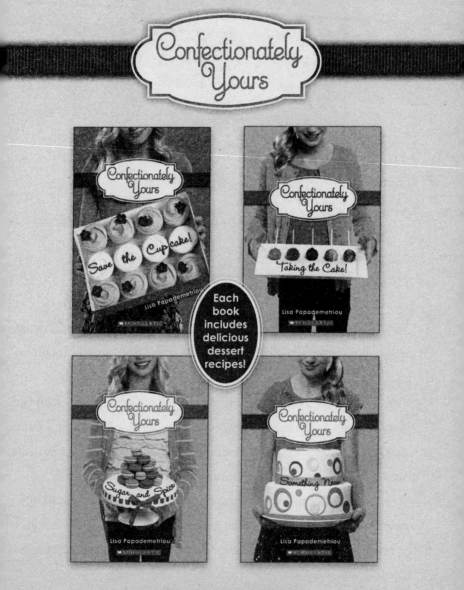

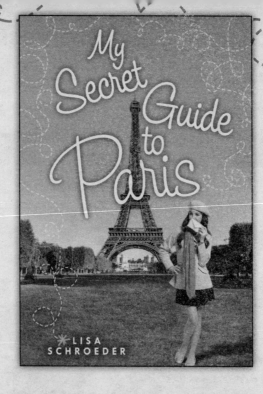

My
Secret Guide
to
Paris

LISA
SCHROEDER

*N*ora loves everything about Paris, from the Eiffel Tower to *chocolat chaud*. Of course, she's never actually been there — she's only visited through her Grandma Sylvia's stories. And just when they've finally planned a trip together, Grandma Sylvia is suddenly gone, taking Nora's dreams with her.

Nora is crushed. She misses her grandmother terribly, but she still wants to see the city they both loved. So when Nora finds letters and a Paris treasure map among her Grandma Sylvia's things, she dares to dream again . . .

She's not sure what her grandma wants her to find, but Nora knows there are wonderful surprises waiting for her in Paris. And maybe, amongst the croissants and *macarons*, she'll even find a way to heal her broken heart.